Snow Globe

Snow Globe
And other stories

Monica Mendoza

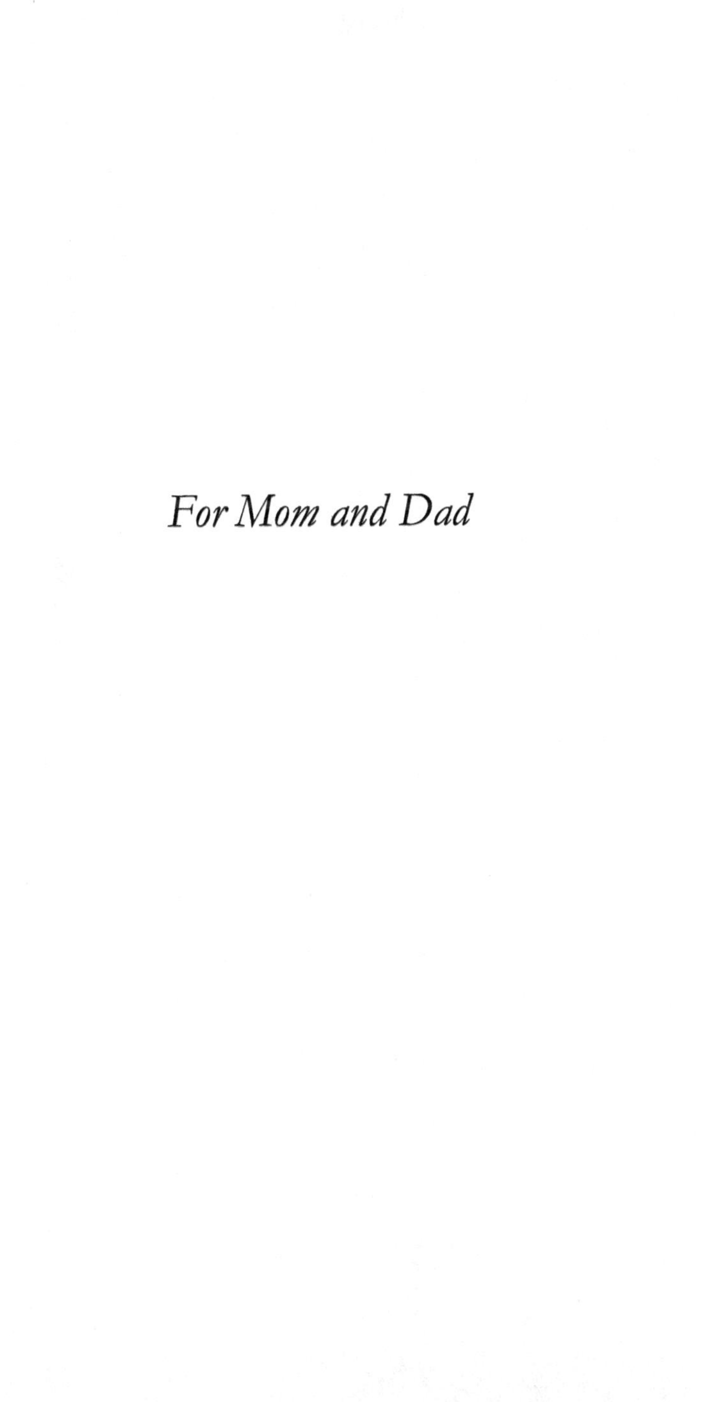

For Mom and Dad

Table of Contents

1. The Umbrella Lady.....................1
2. In Remembrance of Muna Nielsen...11
3. Rosamunde...........................23
4. The Temperament of Starlight.........31
5. Snow Globe.........................39
6. Der Rosenwalzer.....................65
7. Bones in the Forest.................103
8. When the Moon Disappeared.........119
9. The Masquerade....................129
10. Angels.............................149
11. People Who Touch Garbage.........175
12. William Hoyle's Shop of Arcana.....207
13. Flashlight Story....................221

The Umbrella Lady

The city I live in is supposedly haunted by the most polite and beautiful ghost. They call her the Umbrella Lady, and the story goes like this.

Whenever it rains, she appears, shielding herself from the deluge with a white and blue umbrella. Or a red one, or a black one. That detail depends on who's telling the story. It doesn't really matter.

The gist of it is, Umbrella Lady meanders around the city doing good deeds for people and sometimes even changing their lives for the better. I never really paid attention to the story, it was just something that kids at a playground made up or something. One of the many urban legends in the city. If a city is big enough, it's bound to have some ghosts, imaginary or otherwise. There was no reason to believe that story, or even to pay attention to it.

Of course, you must've guessed by now that I have had an encounter with this supposed ghost. Why else would I be bringing all of this up? But the thing is, even now, I'm not sure.

It was a dark and rainy Saturday, and I was heading out with my laptop in my bag to go do work at a café. My dorm's wifi was terrible, especially with the rainstorm that had been going on for the better part of two days. I figured it would be nice to have hot chocolate and fill out yet another resume somewhere that wasn't my messy dorm.

I had originally planned on leaving at 11, but I had spent too much time lying around in bed, so it was actually closer to 12:30 when I finally left the apartment community. The wind sent rain flying like little needles, and very quickly the green, threadbare hoodie I was wearing was soaked. Then as I stepped off the sidewalk to cross the street, my right foot plunged into a deep puddle.

I stood there for a moment, staring at my submerged foot with a mix of surprise and dejection. The people behind me brushed past so they could cross before the little crosswalk light man disappeared and was replaced with a blaring red countdown. A car honked at me as everyone passed by, and I hurried across feeling like a scared mouse. I cursed under my breath and shuddered at the squelching sound that came from my wet shoe with each step.

I walked briskly down the street, hoping that my messenger bag wasn't getting too wet, and that my laptop was okay. I wrapped my fingers around my phone in my front jeans pocket, it was still pumping music through my earbuds so it wasn't hurt by any rain that made it in there. My wallet though... I stopped mid-sidewalk, the flow of foot traffic continuing without me.

I was locked up for a moment, too afraid to check my back pocket because I knew my wallet wasn't there. A sick feeling crept into my stomach as I patted my pocket to confirm that it wasn't there. I checked the other pocket. Then both front pockets, and then the pocket on my hoodie.

Nowhere to be found.

Did I just forget it? Was it currently sitting on my bedside table, or on the kitchen table? Did I drop it, was it buried in the massive laundry pile that sat in the corner of my room?

The sick feeling intensified, and I shuffled off to the side to lean against a railing- I hadn't noticed due to walking with my head down, but I was at the bridge over the river that coursed through the city.

I stared down at the flowing water, the river swollen and full from the February rainfall. It churned angrily, not unlike the acid in my stomach that burned with anxiety.

Maybe it got lost. Maybe it fell out of my pocket and was lying on the sidewalk somewhere, or maybe it fell into a storm drain. Maybe somebody stole it. Maybe, maybe, maybe; my mind was full of maybes and nothing else.

Paralyzed except for compulsively picking at my fingernails and the surrounding skin, the already worrisome idea of a missing wallet was ballooning into a life-ending catastrophe.

I tried so hard to control everything, I had so many rituals that seemed pointless to everyone but were essential to me. But even with all of that, all the mental safeguards I put up and all the habits that my brain promised would keep bad things from happening, here I was. Falling apart.

I think back to this moment and countless others like it and think, I could have avoided so much if I had just retraced my steps, or taken a break from calling myself an idiot and other names, and just breathed. I could have avoided so many meltdowns, so much frustration, so much avoidable turmoil.

But I know it's not my fault that I'm like this.

"You're getting soaked out here! Is everything okay?"

I hadn't heard the footsteps behind me, or even noticed that something was now shielding me from the deluge.

I turned and faced the smiling visage of a rather garishly dressed young woman who was holding an umbrella over both of us.

"I-I'm fine."

"I know it's not my business. I just felt bad, like, you looked really distraught."

"It's fine, I think that I got pickpocketed. Maybe. I'm not sure now. Maybe I left it at home, now that I think about it."

"Sounds like you're feeling a little nervous. What were your plans before this happened?"

I was struck by her earnest smile, and the energy in her eyes.

"I was going to the café." I nodded in the direction of the café, which lay down the street from the Calaveras River Bridge.

"That sounds really nice." The woman bobbed back and forth on the balls of her feet, her long pink and green striped skirt swaying around her calves. "I love taking walks. Especially in the rain. But it looks like it caught you by surprise."

"I guess it did, yeah."

"Hmmm…" She was quiet and stood there, still holding the umbrella over my head. "Had a rough week?"

"Yeah, I guess so."

"That's too bad. What do you think you'll do after this?"

I sighed, wondering why she was having such an interest.

"I-I guess I'm going home to find my wallet, if that's where it is."

"Are you going to do anything that's fun? Movies? Food? Maybe buying yourself something fun?"

"If I find my wallet then I'll buy myself a hot chocolate." I replied, wondering why this was her business all of a sudden, but appreciating the interest nonetheless. Usually I was a 'background' sort of guy.

The woman smiled and reached her gloved hand into the pocket of her rust-colored hoodie.

"I forgot that I had this. I think that you need it more than I do." She handed me a packet of hot cocoa mix, as if that was a perfectly normal thing to have in one's pocket.

"My name is Zoe by the way. What's yours?"

"Oh… My name is Anders."

Zoe held out her hand and shook mine.

"Get yourself somewhere warm, Anders. And give somebody you like a call. See ya later!"

With that she strolled off into the dark early afternoon.

Standing by the railing, holding my new pack of cocoa still in my outstretched hand I was feeling a little stunned. As if that hadn't just happened. As anxious as I had felt a few minutes ago, I now had the urge to follow her. I'm not entirely sure why. I think I was just curious, and wondering if I had just met the ghost.

So I followed the blue and white umbrella.

She strolled slowly but with aim, and entered the shopping district. She carefully hopped around puddles, since she was wearing regular sneakers that probably let in water.

In front of a bookstore sat a homeless man. I can't remember what his cardboard sign said, but it was the usual. Anything helps, God Bless, Lost my Job, I'm a Veteran…

Like I usually did, I'm sorry to say that I avoided eye contact and hastened my pace when I saw him up ahead.

Zoe on the other hand, walked right up to him and held her umbrella over his head.

"Thanks." he muttered.

"No prob. How's your day?"

The man laughed.

"Not so great, but thanks."

"I hope things get better. I know it doesn't help much, but you should have this."

She handed him $20.

"Thanks. It does help."

"I'm Zoe. It was nice to meet you." Zoe shook his hand.

As she walked away, the man looked in his hand in amazement.

"What is it?" I asked him.

"She left me with a hundred more bucks. Must be loaded."

"That's awesome."

I kept following.

A lady was walking down the sidewalk, shopping with her kids- a baby in a stroller and a toddler. A car driving down the street hit a deep puddle and sprayed the water up at them, but Zoe quickly dove forward and blocked the deluge with the umbrella.

"Oh wow! Great reflexes! That would've been bad, Manny, say thank you!"

Her perplexed toddler waved vacantly.

As Zoe walked, she greeted everyone with a smile.

We ended up in the residential area. The front door of an apartment building opened, and a young man in a suit with a briefcase stepped out. When he saw the rain, his shoulders drooped and he held the briefcase up over his head, about to break into a run.

Zoe ran up from behind him and held the umbrella over the both of them.

"Huh? Uh, thank you."

"The storm won't be much longer, don't worry." she said to him.

"I hope so. I have a job interview in like, five minutes. Otherwise I'd have run upstairs to get my jacket."

"I figured you were going somewhere important, you look very nice. Very sharp."

"Thanks. Are… are you really walking me over there?"

Zoe shrugged.

"Where's 'there'?"

"Just some accounting firm down the block a ways."

"Then sure, I don't want your nice suit to get all wet."

The man smiled, and his shoulders relaxed.

"This is it, thanks so much! Have a great rest of your day!"

He stepped in, dry and professional.

The rain was starting to let up. Zoe kept walking towards the street corner.

She turned and saw me. There was no surprise in her eyes. It was as if she knew and didn't care that I had been following the whole time.

I opened my mouth to apologize. I felt hot and awkward. Why had I done that?

She winked and called over the rain and street noise.

"Go make your cocoa!"

Zoe rounded the corner, just as the rain stopped.

After some hesitation I followed, but as I went around the corner, I saw that she was gone. There were many shops and restaurants on that street, and she could have easily ducked into one.

In the end though, I didn't want to know if it was the ghost or not. Maybe it was the ghost, or maybe it was just a very nice woman. Either way, I thought it would be better to let it be.

I went home, found my wallet, and made my hot cocoa.

In Remembrance of Muna Nielsen

It's on kind of a seedy street, but the Nielsen Used Bookstore was August Brodersen's favorite place. It was always pleasant smelling for starters. The smell of used books is like nothing else. It's an old, vaguely woodsy smell- and in a cluttered labyrinth of bookshelves, the smell completes the feel of being in an ancient forest filled with stories.

Even before you lost yourself willingly in the maze of books, the store was enticing.

A tea kettle on a hot plate was always full of warm water. For a little bit of pocket change, you could have a cup of tea or cocoa in a foam cup- the only rule being that you keep the drink in the front area away from the books.

The two tables near the large front window were pleasant, but August's favorite place had always been the lounge. The lounge was a clear area with a sofa, two lounge chairs, and a coffee table. Next to the sofa was a cat tree- because this place wasn't only home to books, but also home to the cats owned by

Mr. Nielsen and his family. In addition, classical music always played from various speakers and it was a great feeling to sit on the sofa and listen, surrounded by cats and music.

Books, music, hot drinks, and cats- what more do you need for a perfect afternoon?

August Brodersen was in need of one such afternoon on a blustery, rainy Saturday.

He already had several books at home that he was planning to read, and several others that he was in the process of reading. Maybe he wouldn't buy anything this time. Maybe he'd just hang out and visit the cats.

"*Hej*, welcome." said a woman's voice in the kind of bored sing-song voice that one acquires for oft repeated phrases.

"*Hej*." August replied, glancing in passing at the woman at the counter. Her cheeks flushed pink and she quickly looked back down at her books.

August browsed the bookshelves. He wasn't really looking for anything in particular. What he wanted was something to kill an afternoon reading in the lounge.

Classics. August had read all sorts in high school, but hadn't really enjoyed them, since they were assigned. August felt weight in his arms and realized that he was already carrying three titles. He didn't remember picking them out, and glanced at the empty spaces on the shelf.

"The Brothers Karamazov, North and South, Our Mutual Friend…"

He didn't think much of it. August found himself spacing out every now and then- not while driving or at work or anything like that, just little bits here and there.

Sauntering off to the science fiction, August felt the weight in his arms increase slightly.

"The Haunting of Hill House."

Looking up he noticed an empty space on the horror shelf.

"Not really into horror, but no harm in giving it a try." He muttered to himself.

August found an old copy of Dune in the Sci-Fi section.

"Oh awesome. The original cover from 1965." a cat brushed softly against August's leg.

"What do you think, buddy?" he said, crouching down to scratch the cat's ears. "I think it's a good price, should I get it?"

The cat, a lovely orange and white creature, purred loudly and playfully pawed at August's hand.

"Her name is Rosmarin."

Looking up, August saw a woman with an armful of books. She had a little nametag on her red, long-sleeved blouse.

MUNA, it read.

"You work here?"

"Yep." she replied, kneeling down next to Rosmarin and putting her books down gently.

"I actually named this cat. Like, eight years ago, I think."

"Really? That's nice, no wonder she likes you so much!"

"Yeah." Muna smiled and stroked the cat affectionately. "So tell me, what books do you have today?"

"Oh, well, I guess I've picked up a few classics, um, a horror story, and this awesome copy of Dune- it has the original cover, first printing. It's in English, though."

"That's very cool. Sounds like a fun selection."

"Yeah, I guess that I just felt like grabbing a bunch and sampling them over in the lounge. Though for sure I want the copy of Dune, it's my favorite book. I already have a copy at home, but… it's kind of silly, but I have one my dad gave me, a cheap one I actually read, and then this one would be so cool to display."

Muna smiled, and was looking at him with a gaze that made him feel… Well, he couldn't quite put his finger on it.

"Sorry… it's uh, kind of weird that I took off ranting like that." August said, and felt himself turning pink.

"Hey, no worries. I work in a bookstore; I see a lot of people who are enthusiastic about books. Last year I saw two people having a heated argument about the best order to read the Narnia books in."

Rosmarin fell asleep on Muna's lap.

"Last year, huh? How long have you been working here?"

"I um… I've been working here for a couple of years. Since I graduated."

She stood up, gently placing Rosmarin back on the ground.

"You probably just don't remember me." Before August could reply, Muna disappeared around a corner and was lost to the shelves.

August sat down in the lounge with his stack of books.

He flipped through the pages of each one, examining the font, the subtle shade of the pages, the texture of the covers- each one was different.

"Which one will you read first?"

A woman with short black hair and pale skin sat down in a lounge chair across from the sofa that August sat on. She wore a black skirt, which she smoothed out as she situated herself on the chair.

"Um… I don't know. Might try this one." he held up The Haunting of Hill House.

"I've read that one. It's excellent."

The woman removed the long, green cardigan she was wearing. There was a heating vent in the lounge, so it was a bit warmer there than other places in the shop.
Under the cardigan she was wearing a red blouse with white flowers on it. She had a name tag that read MUNA.

"Have you read that many horror novels?"

August shook his head.

"Haven't. I think that I'm more of a science fiction guy, myself."

"Right, right, would explain that doorstop." Muna gestured at the copy of Dune.

"Have you read it?" August asked. Muna shook her head.

"I'd like to. Just never gotten around to it."

"If you get the chance, it's really worth the length- y'know, if you ever want to.

"Yeah, it's good to branch out."

August nodded and picked up the horror novel again.

"So, is it nice to work here? If I can ask?"

"Oh, it's a great place to work. It's not all relaxing and reading though. I have to lift a lot of heavy boxes, and organize the books, and I have to climb the stepladder for the top shelf since my dad's been having balance issues."

"Your dad works here too?"

She nodded and began to fiddle with a loose thread on her sleeve cuff.

"Actually, my dad's the owner. So yeah, he works here." she chuckled with an edge of unease.

Muna stared off into space, not trying to make any more eye contact.

"That's cool, I've never seen you before. Have you been away at school?"

"Yeah. Been away. I'll leave you with your books. Talk later."

August spent about an hour sampling the pickings of the day.

Eventually he settled on buying the horror novel along with Dune. He was in the mood to try something new, and besides. It was a mass market paperback, not too expensive. He brought his books to the counter and pulled his wallet out of his back pocket.

"Good choices."

August read the nametag pinned to the cashier's red blouse.

MUNA

"Thanks, how's your day?"

Muna took the books and entered the prices.

"It's fine. How're you paying?"

August handed her a crumpled bill, which she took without looking at him.

"Enjoy, this one's good." she tapped the cover of The Haunting of Hill House.

"You'll like it."

August smiled warmly and watched as she opened each book and put in one of the free little bookmarks.

"Thanks, have a nice day." August said, taking them up off the counter.

"Wait."

August looked back up.

"Do you… want a cocoa or tea?"

Opening his mouth, August was a tad confused.

"Uh…"

"Y-you don't have to, it's just that you have a bit of change. If you want you could use it on a drink… if you want."

"I don't have anywhere I have to be."

Her face lit up.

"Stay right there. I'll make us drinks. Cocoa or tea? I have lemon ginger, Rooibos, Mint, Berry-"

"I like cocoa, that sounds nice."

"Awesome. Stay right there, we can drink them in the lounge, and hang out with the cats."

August leaned his elbows on the counter and watched with bemusement as Muna eagerly opened the cabinet which housed the drinks and biscuits.

There was already water in the pot, so it didn't take long to mix up the two hot chocolates.

"Follow me." Muna had a small tray with two mugs and a little plate of biscuits.

"Wow, um, thanks for the snack." August said as he sat down and Muna placed the tray down on the coffee table.

"You're welcome." there was music in her voice- such a contrast to the bored tones she had been speaking with before.

August sat and took a few sips. It was very rich, chocolatey- he could feel it warming him up.

Muna looked over August's shoulder and did a small wave.

"I'm taking my break now."

August turned and saw a rather absent-minded man wave back. He had the same straight black hair, only his had steely gray streaks. August recognized him as the owner.

"That's my dad." she said, gesturing to the man as he walked out of the room.

"Oh wow, I've never seen you here before, how long have you worked here?"

"A few years. I've always hung out here, though. Since I was a kid. I'm the one who named all the cats." as she spoke, Muna put her mug on the table and picked up an orange and white cat.

"She's called Rosmarin. I remember when she was a kitten."

"That's weird that I've never bumped into you here before. But um, what kind of books do you like? You said that the Hill House book was good."

Muna nodded, burying her face in the cat's soft fur.

"I like horror. I find it explores a lot of really interesting ideas, and that if well done it does a great job of examining the characters- their personalities and how they react to what scares them, and what they prioritize above all else when push comes to shove."

"Huh, when you put it that way it sounds really cool."

"Yeah. I think that you get to know characters very well based on what they're afraid of."

Taking a biscuit from the tray, August saw her hands and noticed that they were trembling and sweaty.

"Hey um, are you okay? If you don't mind my asking."

"I'm good." Muna replied, nuzzling the cat as if for comfort. "I just um… I come off a little strong, but I… you seem cool. Let's keep talking about books. Tell me again about Dune, and how you-"

"Sorry, 'again' about Dune?"

"-how you have two copies, one from your dad and one regular one and how you keep the one from your dad on your shelf, and how you haven't read it since he died-"

August felt himself jump up, spilling hot chocolate on the floor.

"This is getting scary, and I don't like it. Stop it."

Muna also stood up, still holding Rosmarin. Her eyes had tears, just on the brink of spilling.

"I'm sorry. I'm sorry. I'm just- I'm so tired of you coming here and forgetting me the moment I'm out of sight."

"Muna." came the voice of the owner. He was calm. "Muna, take a deep breath."

Muna took a deep, shaky breath.

"I knew you'd love the original cover. I put it on the shelf after I saw you come in. I helped you pick out those other books, too. You said you wanted to try some new books- and I- I just wanted you to stay longer. So we could talk about books."

"I- I don't understand any of this." August felt his own eyes begin to sting.

"I'm sorry. I don't believe any of this."

August flew through the door, out into the wind and rain. He slowed to a brisk walk and pulled his hood up.

He smiled down at the two books in his arms and stuffed them into his jacket.

~*~

Back in the shop, Muna sat on the couch with her cat, crying silently while her father stood with his hand on her shoulder.

In his other hand he held a crumpled letter from himself to himself.

Muna is your daughter, you love her very much. Make every second count, and keep her in your mind as long as you can before you forget.

"I've told him about Rosmarin I don't know how many times." Muna whispered, wiping away the last of the tears.

Mr. Nielsen nodded.

"I know. But next week he'll be back, and you can talk about books again, if you like."

~*~

August hopped into his car and exhaled. He was soaking from the rain, but didn't mind. He brushed his hair out of his eyes and inspected the books. They were perfectly dry, to August's relief.

He opened up Dune.

On the title page, something was written in blue ink.

I know you'll love this. I look forward to falling in love together all over again.
Love,
Muna

"I wonder who Muna was."

Rosamunde

April 11th, 1838

My Felix-

It had been twelve years to the day, dearest. I returned to the countryside where we had lived- in that beautiful mansion that I've told you about. After it burned, there wasn't enough money to rebuild. We moved instead to a smaller house in the city. The house that you know, with the tiny garden, and the piano I play for you. Do you remember the time the window was open, and I played you the newest nocturne by Chopin, and the cheerful sounds of the streets below drifted into the parlor? It's one of my favorite memories, and I hope it's one of yours, too.

The day I returned to Singvogel Mansion, it was raining lightly. I tied Otto to the fence, and he waited patiently for me, with his gentle horse's eyes entreating me to return soon. I know you love my

Otto, rest assured that he had a pleasant journey. I believe he prefers the city, however.

The house didn't completely burn down, the structure is there, it's just too damaged to fix with the money we have. The doors and windows on the ground floor were boarded up, so I didn't even go for the front doors.

Being there brought back a lot of memories. When I was a girl I used to sneak out at night. I climbed down the house out of my bedroom using the lattice we grew flowers on. I always tended religiously to those flowers during the day. If they noticed how trampled the flowers got, I was sure to be discovered. My governess, Annabell, thought I was simply dedicated to my gardening.

I walked through the now overgrown gardens. My boots and the hem of my dress were getting muddy. I remembered the little stone path we once had, but it was overgrown and had sunken into the mud.

I found the wall with my old bedroom window. The lattice had long since fallen, covered in the dried husks of the flowers. I wouldn't be able to climb up into my room as easily as I had hoped. Looking up, I could see the tattered curtains lazily drifting in the air. I remember the last night I ever used the lattice- the night of the fire. I remember my bare feet touching down on the earth, my heart pounding as I realized that I had left my beloved Rosamunde up there. By the time I realized, my father found me and pulled me away from the fire.

Rosamunde

Now, twelve years later, I was coming back to find my Rosamunde- without even knowing whether or not my tiny china lady even survived.

Praying it was rotten enough, I pressed on the wood boarding a first floor window. It gave a bit. I had brought in my bag an assortment of useful things, one of them being a poker from the fireplace. With it, I was able to pry the wood away, and I also cleared away the remainder of glass shards from the windowsill.

Inside, only a little gray sunlight made it inside. Rainwater dripped from the ceiling and patted on my head. I looked up and saw holes in the ceiling-collapsed pieces of the floor from the second story. My eyes adjusted to the light and I took in the sight of the old and decrepit kitchen. Though it had been years, I still knew my way around the mansion. I grew up here, and you never completely forget the home you grew up in.

I took from my bag a small lantern, and lit the candle inside. I was careful, I blew out the match and set it down in a puddle on the concave counter.

In the hallways, no sunlight entered, and the lantern didn't shed much light. My free hand groped along the wall. I remembered a game I used to play with my little cousin Johann on rainy days. You had to shut your eyes and walk through the house looking for the other, relying only on sounds to find your way. The game was my idea, but I didn't get in trouble when poor little Johann fell down the stairs. Even now, not even my dear, crippled, Johann suspects that it was my fault. He was only six, after all. I walked with care up those steps he once tumbled down, careful not to trip on debris.

I reached the top of the steps, and I turned around to look at the beautiful foyer. Even ravaged by fire, I still thought it looked beautiful, if in a rather sad way. It was like a ghost of the house I grew up in. I needed no light to find my way to my old bedroom. I had left the door closed the night of the fire, I remember. I had been sure to close it behind me that night. Pieces of the door were missing, burned away. The door opened easily, thought it felt like it would fall right off the hinges.

Everything looks particularly strange after a fire. I have always been fascinated. I used to take a little magnifying glass and burn patterns into leaves. My old room was exactly how I remembered it, but marked by the fire. My bed was charred, the sheets were gone, the mattress partially burnt away. My wardrobe hung open, my old dresses and coats were blackened and fragile. I ran my fingers across a once pink party dress, and my fingers were dirtied with ash.

On my bed were the remains of a stuffed rabbit, I believe his name was Fritz. I turned to my bookcase and saw the singed spines of my favorite books. I had the feeling that if I picked one up it would disintegrate in my hands. It's like my childhood was trapped in amber, and the slightest movement would shatter it. I hardly dared to even breathe too loudly.

I remember the night of the fire, I was nine years old. I was playing at night like I always did, but I had a little chill, so I didn't want to climb down to the gardens. Instead, Rosamunde and I would play hide and seek. I placed her under the bed- she would hide first. My imagination made up for her lack of movement, and I went off to count in the foyer.

I had the layout of the mansion memorized, I didn't have to light my way with a candle. Felix, did you ever sneak around your house at night? It seems like a completely different place, does it not? I used to imagine my nocturnal house was in a different world than my sunlit house. In the nocturnal world, there were faeries and monsters, but they wouldn't bother me tonight. The creatures from my mind always respected me when I was in the middle of a game. Lightly I tiptoed down the stairs, and when I reached the bottom I pressed my face against the post at the bottom of the banister and counted to ten. Rosamunde didn't need that much time to hide, since she was so small.

Twelve years later, I lifted the burnt bedsheets away from the floor and peered into the space underneath. Once upon a time, I would've imagined a creature hiding under here, but now there was nothing underneath except what remained of my Rosamunde. Her clothes and hair were burnt, and the paint on her face was nearly gone. Yet, she was my Rosamunde, who I had come back for. For some reason, I came back here for this relic.

I left my room and walked down the hall- I arrived at the stairs and my heart began to pound. See, I hadn't revisited this memory for a long time and it had faded gray in my mind. Slowly descending the stairs, I remembered in such vivid detail and I felt as if my heart would burst out of me.

I was counting. Over the years I had become comfortable with my nighttime adventures. I knew how much noise I could make without waking people up, but I hadn't thought that my governess, Annabell, would be up and about as well that night. She got up at night and lit herself a lamp. She heard whispering in the foyer, came to investigate, and saw the small white shape at the bottom of the stairs. My poor, superstitious governess Annabell. She thought I was a spirit, maybe. Maybe she was just coming down the stairs and tripped. What I know is that when Annabell fell and broke her neck, the lamp shattered on the rug and it went ablaze.

I ran. I ran, Felix. I ran to my room and hid under the covers, praying that Annabell was alive, and that the fire would extinguish itself. I had just wanted to play at night. Just like I had simply wanted to play when it was Johann who fell down those stairs. At first, I thought it was the stairs that were cursed. In time, I believed that it was a blessing for the house to burn down. But as I descended them one last time with Rosamunde in my arms, I finally accepted that the problem is not the stairs. The problem is me.

Johann cannot walk because of the silly game I made up, and Annabell snapped her neck because I got up at night to play. You, my dear Felix, lie asleep for what is now the fourth day after the accident. You were crossing the street after visiting me on a foggy Sunday, and when you were halfway across I called for your attention, I don't even remember what for now. You never saw the carriage coming, and if you wake up, I doubt you will remember. I trace it back to the games in the old mansion. Something is wrong about me, and I don't know what. I have no clue who this curse of mine will take next, but I'm sorry that it had to be you.

Know that I will forever love you, even if I am the one who caused this.

Yours forever,

Augusta Kalterberg

The Temperament of Starlight

It had been years- yes, fifteen years, since Diana had even thought about that night. What was supposedly unforgettable had simply vanished from mind until that quiet, hot, afternoon.

They were selling the cabin. That cabin possessed the memories of so many summers. Arguments with her brothers, games of hide and seek, and running, wet and slippery-fresh off the lake and ready for lunch.

It was a pity to sell the cabin, but as children grow, so do the expenses, and besides, Diana hadn't been there for ages- before college. The last time any family member had been there was when Diana's dad went fishing on the lake and used the cabin for the afternoon. The money would solve some problems, and dad figured he could come and fish at the lake without needing a whole cabin.

Diana drove up from the city as soon as she could after getting the phone call from her mom. She had been away from nature for too long, and though it was sad to say goodbye to the cabin, Diana's heart was full as she drove through the gold tinged woods, and heard the gentle lap of waves on the dark brown shore. Dark brown with flecks of gold.

Diana took the old key out of her pocket, the planks of the patio squeaking underfoot. Startled by the noise, a squirrel darted out from under the porch and scurried up the trunk of a nearby tree.

As usual, the door had to be shoved inward *hard* as one opened it. It brought back memories of slamming against it, reluctant to slow down even for a jammed front door.

Light flooded lazily through the windows, filtered through jaunty yellow curtains. The furniture was still there, covered up with clear plastic sheets to keep spiders and dust away from the upholstery.

Outside, the noise from trees and the water was soft, but present. Indoors though, the only sound was the occasional creak of the floorboards. It felt like time had stopped.

In the hallway, Diana peered into the bedrooms. Her brothers shared the first room down the hall, right next to their parent's room. They had a tendency to get up to mischief at night, but not so much when they knew mom and dad could hear them.

Diana's room was on the opposite side of the hall, and she brushed the attic cord aside and twisted the doorknob. Her door still had a faded construction paper sign on it. She smiled, remembering the time she made that butterfly shaped name card.

Inside were Hello Kitty curtains, that ten minutes slow clock, and the bedframe covered in stickers and marks etched in pencil.

Her mom had told her to go search the house to make sure she had everything that belonged to her. There was nothing to be taken really. Mom said they'd take the furniture, so she didn't have to worry about that. Diana stood on the mattress and took down the curtains, also taking down the faulty clock.

"That's kind of it." she said to nobody.

Turning around though, the sliding closet door caught Diana's eye. A memory of playing hide and seek came back- but also a different memory. One she couldn't quite grasp.

The door slid open with a bit of difficulty. Diana brushed spider web off her hands and knelt down.

There was nothing in the closet except a scarf that was torn, hanging from the beam. On the closet floor there were two shoe boxes. One was marked as "Cool Leaves", the other was unmarked, and shoved far back in a dark and dusty corner. Diana tossed the lightweight leaf box aside and reached into the closet for the unmarked one.

It was unexpectedly heavy and there was the feeling of something rolling from one side to the other. Diana heard a sloshing water sound, and memories of a deep blue indigo filled her mind.

The lid came off easily, tearing a few ancient spiderwebs.

Inside the shoebox was an artifact of a night Diana couldn't believe she had ever forgotten.

Diana was always happily exhausted at the end of the day. Usually, she fell asleep right away, but tonight something woke her before she could fall asleep completely.

They called it Pleiades Lake. At night, the sky was studded with stars and the same stars were reflected in the calmness of the water's surface. Sometimes dad remembered the telescope and they set it up for stargazing.

That night, a glimmer of light streaking across the sky caught her interest through the slightly parted curtains. This light, far brighter than a shooting star, piqued Diana's interest in a way that overrode all fatigue. The night was warm; she threw off the sheets and threw open the curtains.

The bright lights gracefully arched across the sky, landing on the lake, skittering across the water like skipping stones before sinking into the water and extinguishing after a while.

Her breath taken away, Diana's eyes widened as she watched, sliding up the window.

The noise was soft. When a star hit the water it was with a gentle bell and splash sound. No terrifying thuds or booms.

She *needed* a closer look. As softly as she could, Diana popped out the screen and stuck her head out the window. The beautiful lights beckoned- just by *being*. At eleven years old, Diana had read many books about marine light. She thought about Anglerfish, and how they lured hapless prey with a beautiful light attached to their head.

She wondered, am I about to be swallowed by a massive leviathan? Or is the lake itself a monster?

Pushed past fear by curiosity, Diana climbed onto the windowsill and hopped onto the knee-tall grass around the cabin.

Slowly she walked, pausing behind trees, but never being satisfied with the view.

Closer. Closer.

The waves on the shore were no bigger than usual. As they sank, the stars seemed to disrupt no water.

Diana felt the water around her ankles, her feet sinking into the silt. Even out in the water, the dance of stars still called to her.

She waded out further- the water sloshed around her pajama pants at the knee. The middle of the lake was over twenty feet deep- that was where the stars were dancing, though!

Diana turned back to shore, where one of the kayaks was tied up. Diana climbed in and untied it. She clumsily rowed through the dark water, toward the center of the lake.

A star skipped along the water- close to the kayak. Diana watched as the star sank into the depths- illuminating the water with a soft, white blue light.

Another star sank down- a brilliant white light with a yellow glow.

As she rowed into the center, she noticed the different colors- and the patterns that the stars made with their tails as they skipped along the lake. And she noticed- the dance continued under the water. The stars underwater coordinated and moved in sync with those above, and the skipping stars complimented this with their movement.

Now in the center of the lake, Diana ceased rowing. The kayak floated freely on the water.

The depths were like a dark sapphire, but the stars illuminated the water like fireworks.

The underwater stars, the surface stars, and the airborne stars all aligned and paused, as if waiting for a musical cue only they could hear. Diana, in the middle of this wide circle, held her breath, eyes wide with anticipation.

The underwater stars rushed upward and broke the surface, water splashing and small waves rocking the kayak. The water as part of the dance- the droplets displaced were suspended in air, tossed between stars and creating beautiful shapes.

Diana felt water droplets drizzle on her head, and realized that the water was falling back down to the lake- no longer suspended in air. The stars surrounding her were in the formation of a spring- winding up to the sky like a spiral staircase. Moving gracefully, the stars returned back to their home in the sky.

The glare from starlight reflected in the water caught Diana's eye.

One by one, as each star returned, the glimmers of light vanished from the water.

A strange impulse overtook Diana. She grabbed a water bottle from the bottom of the kayak.

She unscrewed the cap and dumped the iced tea into the bottom of the boat. Leaning out of the kayak, Diana reached her arm out as far as it would go, scooping up the starlit water with the bottle. Diana tumbled back into the kayak, rocking it and sending ripples out into the lake.

The water in the bottle emitted a soft, blue-white glow- as if it was at once water and pure illumination.

The last of the stars disappeared. The lake stretched out, wide, deep, and dark. Alone in the center was a kayak floating freely, with Diana and her glowing bottle of starlight. She stared at it in silence- expecting it to fade- but it never did. Diana screwed the lid back on, and it took a moment for her eyes to adjust to the night.

Rowing back carefully, Diana had the bottle firmly between her feet, not daring to let the bottle roll around on the floor.

After tying the boat up, Diana did not run back to her window. She walked, carrying the bottle gingerly.

A safe place. A safe place for the bottle of starlight.

Indigo memory gave way to orange present. The sun sent warmth streaming through the window, bringing Diana back to herself, in the moment.

She held the bottle in her hands, the cap next to her on the floor.

The starlight was no less dim than it was the night the stars danced. Diana replaced the cap and smiled ear to ear. Her dad's old metal water bottle.

That summer, years ago, he was disappointed that it was lost. He just assumed that it fell out of the kayak.

Diana rolled up the curtains and placed them in the box- and gently rested the bottle on top. She replaced the lid on the old shoebox.

Carefully, Diana loaded the boxes and other miscellaneous items into her car, and took one last lingering look at the lake, before turning the key in the ignition and driving away.

She'd come back someday.

Snow Globe

Though the last scrap of the universe was moments away from vanishing, Attens-Rekka was fussing over the prince. She polished the glass case he slept in and pulled aside the curtain she had placed over the blasted-out chunk of the wall. She swept the heavy carpet of dust and dirt off the floor, and cleared the tall, tri-fold mirror in the corner.

In the mirror, Rekka brushed dust off her tattered dress, with one fully flesh covered hand and one hand with skeletal metal fingers. With a small cloth that hung over the top of the mirror, Rekka polished the silver brooch that pinned her sash to her dress, and proceeded to polish all the circular metal ornaments that decorated her asymmetrical neckline. With artificial tears, she cleared dust from her eyes that she hadn't even noticed were disrupting her vision, and combed her hair with her fingers until it was satisfactory.

After that moment making sure she was presentable, Rekka went back to fixing the room.

She swept up the shards of a broken vase, picked up and straightened out an old chair with an embroidered back, and replaced the books that had fallen off the shelf.

The prince's bookshelf spanned the entire wall, and Rekka remembered that centuries ago, the queen would often take a book off the shelf, sit in the embroidered chair, and read to the prince as he lay in stasis.

As Attens-Rekka picked up the last book that had been shaken off the shelf by a tremor, she realized that she hadn't read to the prince in a good while. Though he was kept in stasis, Rekka had been instructed to occasionally read to Hugo. It was thought that perhaps he could, to some extent, hear when they were speaking to him, and the queen was awfully worried that he would somehow be bored or lonely.

Rekka sat down in the embroidered chair and opened the book. Though she had all of Hugo's favorite books memorized, Rekka found the process of reading aloud from the page to be much more "authentic" and "human" than simply reciting it like it was data. The queen, she had been able to recite songs and stories from heart in a way that sounded warm and natural, but Rekka hadn't quite gotten the hang of it yet.

The pages of the book were fragile in Rekka's hands, and flakes of gold leaf adhered to her fingertips as she turned the pages. As she reached the end of the book, the final pages started to crumble from their sheer age. Flakes of paper, gold leaf, and dried ink rose into the air like smoke and joined the dust that stubbornly covered the chamber.

Rekka closed the book without finishing the story, the final page having disintegrated. She had the ending memorized, of course, but said nothing. She merely placed the book back in its place on the shelf and turned her face back to the open wall. At least it was quiet. What lovely golden hours they had there.

This was a safe place. A safe place with a generator powered by crystals that could supply energy for centuries. A similar crystal lay in the heart of Rekka, and it was for the want of such a crystal that the war between two empires ended in the eradication of both.

This was a sanctuary like no other. Which is what made it so peculiar when a knock sounded on the door of the chamber.

The absurdity of knocking on the front door of ruins wasn't lost on Gaia. But if her endless days of wandering the universe had taught her anything, it was that one should never barge into a place, no matter how decrepit or deserted it looks. Doing so is just inviting trouble from the potential resident who got there first.

This structure was carved out of a floating chunk of rock near the last star, and looked like some kind of chapel. It was surrounded by a translucent shimmer that was familiar, some kind of old barrier technology that hadn't been seen for centuries. Gaia's transport was parked at the edge of the short length of pathway that had been left in front of the heavy, chrome doors. Upon landing and stepping out of her pretty much defunct transport, Gaia had been half expecting to suffocate and burn in the vacuum of space, but the old barrier technology held up. This structure must've dated back to at least the Dual Empire Era.

The exterior decoration was practically non-existent, though. Dual Empire Era aesthetics almost *required* flashy decoration of every kind. Statues, tapestries, flying buttresses, and elaborate mosaics were all stapes of that era, even on the more modest structures.

When *was* that door going to open? Gaia was about to examine the doors further to find a way in when they actually opened. The chrome door shuddered upward with a mechanical whir, revealing the occupant of the desolate ruins.

She was a robot, and judging by her elegant albeit damaged clothes, she looked like a servant of a royal court. Gaia could tell that she had been meant to be beautiful, and probably was at one time, but was rather hideously disfigured; one half of her head looked like a youthful woman with flowing brown hair, and the other half of her head was little more than a metal skull, though miraculously both of her silver eyes were intact. This duality extended to her arms, one of which was soft and fully fleshed while the other was skeletal. Gaia had seen worse though and wasn't shaken.

She stepped in through the door, pulled down her black hood and kicked the dust off her boots.

"Took you long enough to answer the door, who did you think it was?" Gaia asked.

"How did you find this place?" the robot asked in a soft, pleasing voice, pulling the lever to shut the door.

"There's nobody alive who knows the location of this chamber."

Gaia shook her head and smiled.

"The edges of the universe pretty much had me cornered. It's not that I was trying to find your hideout. It's just that this little rock is pretty much the last place there is." She took off her cloak, showing her black, strapless dress. The robot said nothing, and continued to regard her guest with bemusement.

"There really is nothing left." said Gaia again. Was the robot not listening?

"I wasn't aware. I had a vague inkling that the rest of the universe had fallen into ruin. I didn't know the extent of it, however."

"Refresh my memory, who are you? And since the world is such a *tiny* place these days, have we met before?" asked Gaia, genuinely unsure if they had met before. The robot shook her head.

"We haven't met. Unless my inner clock is incorrect, I haven't seen a human besides Prince Hugo for... 29,089 years. Unless you are older than that and served on the royal court of the Neptunian Aristocracy."

Gaia laughed as she started to look around the room. The interior certainly *did* suggest Dual Empire Era. In particular, the lovely mosaic floor caught her attention. It looked like a map plotting out the stars of this galaxy.

"29,089 years, and you're still stuck in the days of the Neptunians? As I recall, them and the Pan-Europan Empire destroyed each other." Gaia paused at the glass case, regarding the many cables that snaked into the floor to the crystalline generator hidden below the mosaic tiled floor.

"You said something about a "Hugo". Is this him?"

"Yes." said the robot.

"Prince Hugo Kosmian XI of the Neptunian Royal Family, Second in Line to the Throne."

"To a non-existent throne, you mean. You know, my memory gets awfully fuzzy after a certain amount of time passes, but I remember something about a Prince Hugo. The royal family hid him away during the war, but when everything fell apart, he was still missing. Nobody ever found him. I think he became some kind of urban legend, a holy grail of sorts for archaeologists."

"All that is correct." said the robot, placing her fleshed hand on the case.

"They hid him away, putting him in stasis. Not just because of his illness, too. There was no cure, and he was dying. He was only twelve, the queen was simply distraught. They hid him here with me. I have been his caregiver ever since he was an infant. They stopped visiting. I suppose that's when the war ended.

"... in the destruction of both parties."

"I would assume so." said the robot.

"You said you're a caregiver?"

"Attens-Rekka. Caretaker of Prince Hugo-"

"-Kosmian XI, yes. I don't suppose it matters to a royal caretaker, but I'm Gaia."

"Gaia who?"

"Just Gaia. I think I've always just been Gaia. The *very* earliest memory I have, from billions of years ago, is being named Gaia and living in a place called... I think it was called Rome."

"I haven't heard of that place. Perhaps if I could still access the Universal Database..."

"From what I can recall, it was rather similar to the Pan-Europan Empire, in terms of religion, hierarchy, and culture."

"How interesting." said Rekka, resting her chin on her skeletal hand.

"How can you be so old yet appear as you do?"

"Well..."

There was a flash of light.

It only lasted for a moment- so brief that they might have just dismissed it as a visual trick, a glint of fading sunlight reflecting off the mirror.

But standing by the blasted-out wall was a man. A very confused looking man.

"Huh? Where am I this time? Is this as far as I can go?" Edgar said to himself rather disoriented and swaying on his feet. For a moment his vision was blurry, and he felt disoriented; Edgar found that his vision frequently needed a few seconds to adjust after a leap.

Edgar blinked once. Twice. He was indoors, in some kind of room. It looked like a room in a castle of some sort, very fancy and well-furnished. But there was something off about it, something so different from the last place he had been.

Standing before him were two women. At least, one of them looked like a normal woman. The other looked like something out of a movie. Her appearance was frightening to him and made his stomach turn, but Edgar knew that they were probably just as shocked, if not more shocked, by his sudden appearance.

"Who are you?" The skeletal woman said in a demanding voice- very human sounding too, in contrast to her appearance. Her manner of speaking was hard for Edgar to understand at first, but it was similar enough to the way people spoke in the previous era he had visited that he figured he'd be able to understand and be understood.

"Oh, my goodness." he said, taking off his hat to be polite, and nodding slightly.

"I- I'm Edgar. Edgar Whitmore. Sorry to come out of nowhere like that, my sincerest apologies um, ladies." he said. Edgar was sure that his words sounded antiquated to their ears, the same way he had a hard time understanding the first few minutes of a Shakespeare play. His clothes probably also looked silly to them. Compared to the dark-haired woman's elegant black dress and the skeletal woman's fancy blue one, he supposed he not only looked quaint, but far too casual for whatever place this was.

When they didn't respond, Edgar tried again. He wanted to at least be polite. He'd encountered many strange places and people while leaping around, and this wasn't the strangest thing he'd popped in on.

"Um, hello ladies. I'm Edgar Whitmore. I can leap through time as my leisure, and today my journey has taken me to your fine, um... place." He said, unsure of *what* exactly this place was supposed to be. Some kind of bedchamber? Except instead of a bed there looked to be a glass coffin. Edgar cleared his throat.

"Well... now that I've introduced myself, how about you two take a turn at it?"

"Um, well... my name is Gaia. I'm over a billion years old, I think, but I still haven't learned how to jump through time."

Edgar's blue eyes widened. He was also having trouble understanding the odd speech of these two beings, but if his ears didn't deceive him, that woman said she was over a *billion* years old.

"Wow, over a billion years old? What year is this, is everyone immortal like that?"

"The year isn't relevant anymore." said the skeletal one.

Edgar's attention turned from the woman in black to the one in blue.

"Who are you? Are you an android or something? Forgive me if I come off as rude, the time

I'm from, 1961, doesn't have anything like you. Any*one* like you, I mean. Sorry."

"I'm Attens-Rekka, caretaker to Prince Hugo Kosmian XI of the Neptunian Royal Family, Second in Line to the Throne-"

"She's very proud of that..." said Gaia, sitting down in the embroidered chair.

"This is certainly a strange situation..." she mused from the chair.

"A robot, a time-traveler, an immortal, and a prince in stasis. Sounds like the set-up of a great joke."

"Prince in stasis?" asked Edgar.

"You mean inside this case is..." Edgar approached the glass case. From the sides, the glass was tinted gold, and so the prince could only be viewed by standing directly in front of the case. Edgar gasped.

"Who is he? What is he the prince of?"

"The Neptunian Alliance of the Twelve Planets. Royalty descended from the people of the Upper Atmosphere Kingdom of Neptune. It was Prince Hugo's ancestors that-"

"I don't think our guest needs a whole history lesson." yawned Gaia.

"Besides, if he's really a time traveler from the most distant past, should we really be giving him spoilers?"

"This future is so distant that I doubt anything I learn would really make much of a difference. Besides, it's not like I would be able to tell anyone." said Edgar, his face falling.

"Why not?" asked Gaia. Edgar hesitated and scratched the back of his head awkwardly.

"Well, you know. People in my time are pretty quick to decide you're loony. Nobody would believe me, not even my own mother, I'd bet."

"How are you able to leap through time?" asked Rekka, intrigued. She still stood protectively by the side of Hugo's case, but didn't seem completely suspicious of the stranger. He was an anomaly, but seemingly benign.

"Ah well, see, I actually don't know. When I was little, if I concentrated *really* hard, I could make the little hands on my dad's watch go backwards all of a sudden, and I thought I was doing it with my mind, like a magician or something. After a while though, it became pretty apparent to me that it wasn't something as simple as just making a watch hand move."

"I've never encountered a person like you." said Gaia.

"Of course, maybe I forgot. I definitely don't remember anything from the 1960s. I remember that they happened, but anything besides that is beyond me."

"So... listen, I've been trying to jump as far forward as I possibly can. Just for fun. Last place I was, it was this *magnificent* golden building, with a stage, and there was this amazing music playing. It sounded like the opera, except that no opera sounded like this stuff. It was heavenly. How long ago was that? Do either of you ladies know a golden building with angelic music? I can't always tell where I am going, geographically, but I try to stay in or around the same place. Would you know about that place?"

Rekka nodded her head.

"I remember the Ionian Opera House. A beautiful display of the wealth of the Neptunian Royal Family."

"I'll give them credit for making their fabulous display of wealth something that we could *all* enjoy. At least from the outside." mused Gaia, fiddling with the bird pendant around her neck.

"Does that place still exist?" Edgar asked, moving away from the case and walking around the chamber. He could tell that it was once very lavish and beautifully decorated, with a shelf full of books that spanned an entire wall, and masterfully crafted furniture, beautiful mosaics on the floor and the ceiling, as well as framed paintings on the walls.

However, there was an air of desolation hanging over the chamber. It reminded Edgar of pictures he had seen in history books, ancient Egyptian tombs filled with priceless treasures and sealed away from the rest of the world.

"I don't believe that place exists anymore." said Gaia.

"I ended up here because there was nowhere else to go. My little vessel was running fumes, anyway."

"Nowhere else to go?"

"This is the last bit of the universe left. Slowly but surely, the walls are closing in. An odd shimmer that distorts and eats up the space- leaving nothing behind. Looking at the edge of it too long has driven people to madness, not like there really are people. I can't remember the last time I actually saw another person besides you two."

"Three. There are three more of us." said Rekka, rather defensively for an elegant robot.

"He's not dead?" asked Edgar incredulously, gesturing at the gilded glass case.

"No, of course not. Not even the royal family would invest such expense in keeping a corpse looking fresh. Prince Hugo was terminally ill during the war, and because there was no cure, they put him into stasis so they could buy some time." explained Rekka.

"They never came back, though?" Edgar asked.

"Is that what happened to everyone? A big war?"

"I don't things were ever the same after the Pan-Europans and the Neptunians destroyed each other. They took a lot of the best technology and culture with them when they kicked it." said Gaia.

Edgar looked down sadly and went to lean against the wall, looking out at the bleak, rocky landscape outside. If he had to guess, he would assume they were lazily drifting on some kind of asteroid near a star that may or may not be the sun he knew.

"So that's how it all ends? After all this time, it's just another war?"

"Well... life went on after the wars, it was just different." said Gaia.

"And the universe was going to be on its way out anyway. If there was more time, then surely people would've rebuilt again. It's just that things weren't meant to reach such heights again."

"Right..."

"Oh, don't be like that. Talking to you, I think I remember a little bit about your time, if just a scrap. How old are you?"

"I'm 27."

"You'd have just been a kid when it was all going down, the war?"

"Yeah, I remember bits and pieces of it. Hiding in the cellar in my mum's garden." he said, hesitating.

"But the present, *your* present, is doing alright." said Gaia. "Not perfect, god no, but life is still happening, right? There was a little stumble, but you all got back up. *We* all got back up, I forget, I was there too. There's something you've gotta understand though. That's not the last time that your civilization is going to be brought to its knees, and that's not even the worst it will be. War is a constant, but thankfully it's not the only constant."

"Thanks." said Edgar glumly. "It's just odd. I focused so hard today, trying to get as far as I possibly could. I wanted to see just how amazing the future got, and for a while it was pretty amazing. It went back and forth like you said just now, but I didn't expect it to end like this. Do you really think it's the end? There couldn't possibly be more?"

"I wouldn't try it if I were you." said Gaia.

"Who knows what'll happen if you try and jump to a time where there's nothing? Where there isn't *even time?*"

"Edgar might disappear if he tries that." said Rekka.

"Granted, neither of us know you or what you can do. But I wouldn't try it. Just assume this is it, and skip on home. Better sooner, rather than later. Who knows how much longer we're going to be safe in this chamber. Nothing can stop the decay, not even these walls." said Gaia, oddly serene given the circumstances.

"I can't go back with this being the last place..." Edgar said, his eyes taking on an odd, golden quality in the waning light.

"Why not?" asked Rekka.

"Yeah, it's not like *you're* trapped here. You've still got a long time."

There was a moment of long silence, the only noise being a soft, almost imperceptible humming noise- the hum of the crystal stored below the tiled floor.

"What about you? And the prince? You're okay with just dying here when it- it finally reaches you?"

Gaia shrugged her bare shoulders.

"Well, I've been alive for a pretty long time, and even though I forget a lot of things after a certain amount of time, I have started to get bored. If anything, this is finally something different. Maybe even exciting."

"I'm the prince's caretaker. There's nothing I'd rather do than attend to him. Even unto the end of the world."

"And what about him?" Edgar asked, turning away from the sunlight and looking at the case with doleful eyes.

"What *about* him?" asked Rekka.

"He will continue to sleep. I was instructed to look after him until there was a cure and he was awakened."

"You do realize that there will never be one though, right?" said Gaia. "It could be a few minutes, it could be another year, but this little rock is pretty much all that is left. If I were Prince Hugo, I would want to be awake for a little while, instead of just disintegrating in my sleep."

"But..." Edgar said hesitatingly.

"Wouldn't that be kind of... frightening? To go to sleep as a prince and wake up on the last asteroid in the universe? In what's basically ruins? I don't know if I would want to face my doom so head on... Maybe it is more merciful to just let him sleep."

"I agree. I don't think that I have the qualifications to handle this situation." said Rekka, rather anxiously for a robot. "I'm much more comfortable simply doing what I was ordered to. Care for the prince until the end. I think that awakening the prince right now would cause him too much distress. Doing this would not be taking care of him at all."

"Well maybe he should at least be given the chance to live a little before everything disappears." said Gaia.

"She has a point." said Edgar, running a hand through his brown hair. "I mean... I would want to at least know. So that I could choose how to spend the time I had left..."

"It isn't your place to decide what to do." said Rekka, somewhat defensively.

Gaia rose from the embroidered-back chair and folded her arms. She strode over to the gilded case and leaned over it. Edgar also stepped a little closer and said,

"Well, it isn't your place either. But since the only person who really has a right to decide is out cold, then I suppose we're at a bit of a stalemate."

"Hmm." said Gaia after a long silence. The long silence persisted afterward, too. Edgar knew there was no wind outside, yet there *was* some kind of noise. His mind wandered off. How were they breathing? Looking out the broken wall, he could see that they were in a structure on an asteroid. There must be some kind of... shield, perhaps. They were like fish in a bowl. Or maybe this is what it was like inside a snow globe. The thought crossed Edgar's mind as he thought about the snow globes in his grandmother's house. He could recall being a very young child, enthralled by them. So proud that grandmother had let him hold one, Edgar gently turned it upside down and watched as snow fell on a tiny city, populated by tiny people. Tiny people who went to the tiny church, and visited the tiny pretzel shop, dressed in their tiny winter coats. Little as he was, Edgar had imagined what it was like to be a tiny person living in the snow globe city.

An odd feeling overtook him as he looked at the other three people. The pale as death prince, with hair and clothes as neat as a corpse, yet still living. The young-looking woman with eyes older than anything he'd ever seen. The decrepit robot, a relic of an older, richer time.

Then, of course, there was him. Just normal Edgar. He had average marks in school, and he had an average job. He didn't have a lot of friends, and he lived with his mother because he had to care for her as she got older. The two of them lived in an average flat, the most unique thing inside being his father's ashes and military award up on the mantlepiece. For a while, he had a girlfriend, but his secret proved too much for her, she thought he was crazy. Ah, his secret. Now that was one thing that was anything but average. Maybe he did fit in with these people, in a strange way.

This nagging feeling didn't let go. This feeling that they *were* little people in a snow globe. Perhaps the disintegration of the universe wasn't the end of everything, maybe it was just the glass breaking.

"We don't know what will happen." said Edgar lowly.

"Huh?" asked Gaia.

"Gaia, you said that you've been trying to outrun the disintegration, but you don't know what it really is."

"I *do* know that it destroys whatever it touches." she said, the memory of that gold-dust mirage on the horizon sending shivers down her spine. Goosebumps formed on her naked arms.

"But what if it's just something we don't understand? Like dying, what if there's something after the disintegration?"

"It's true, we don't know anything about the nature of this phenomenon." said Rekka, after a long time of simply listening to the others talk.

"It could be, that this is only the end of the world that we are familiar with. Perhaps there *is* something beyond. Not that I'm qualified to speculate about any of this." She added the last part hastily.

Gaia stood up and grabbed her cloak, wrapping it around her cold arms. Edgar also shivered, realizing that it had gotten a little more frigid inside the chamber. Shimmering particles of barely visible gold were appearing in the air.

"What do you think, Attens-Rekka, royal caretaker?" Gaia asked with mock sanctimoniousness. The sarcasm didn't seem terribly malicious or belittling, however. Rather, it seemed that Gaia was appealing to the part of Rekka that still clung to ceremony and civilization. After all, the poor caretaker hadn't known anything besides golden halls and other fine things. She hadn't lived through countless wars and plagues or been worn down and wearied by the constant rising and falling of cultures, and most importantly, she hadn't been constantly losing old memories as quickly as she made new ones.

Rekka was, for all ceremony and presumption, a simple, naïve thing.

"I believe... I believe that... the prince would be awful frightened." said Rekka in a soft voice.

"I've been afraid lots of times. It's not the worst thing in the world." replied Gaia.

"But to inflict that on him, knowing full well that he would be scared..."

"Do you know why I'm here?" Edgar asked, walking to Rekka. "I'm here because... last week- for me it was last week- I jumped ahead in time for fun. Just to see if I would win a bet I made about football with my mates. A petty use of my gifts, I know. But do you know what I saw, on the street by the pub I frequent?" Edgar took a deep breath. "I saw myself. I saw myself crushed to a pulp by a bus as I crossed the street. I knew then and there that there was *nothing* I could do. Nothing in the world. I spent the better part of this week sitting around, at a stalemate with myself, you know? I couldn't believe that I would die so abruptly. So... I thought I would look ahead. I wanted to see the future, and I wanted to know everything about it."

Edgar took Rekka's hands- the fleshed one that radiated artificial body heat, and the cold, metal, skeletal one too.

"This isn't what I thought I would find at the very farthest reach of time. But I wouldn't trade it for anything. If I hadn't jumped ahead to look and see if I would win, I wouldn't have been able to get ready. I'd be sitting at home right now eating chips, or at work punching out expense reports. I wouldn't have had the chance to set up support for my mum, I wouldn't have had time to forgive Charlotte... Given the choice, I would rather know."

Rekka's silver eyes shimmered with artificial moisture.

Gaia put a hand on her shoulder, the silken fabric still soft to the touch after all these years.

"Let's wake Hugo."

Rekka nodded.

She leaned down and pressed a small, green gemstone on the side of the case. A control panel rose from the floor, with a keypad and flickering screen. It accepted Rekka's handprint, and the code she entered, fingers flying across the buttons.

There was the sound of air hissing, and the lid of the case retracted, or rather, to Gaia and Edgar's eyes it almost looked like the glass simply vanished.

Hugo's amber eyes blinked open in his gray face. Rekka only had a breathing function to appear lifelike, yet she still quickened her breaths. She knelt by the side of the case as his eyes focused. Gaia looked and Edgar and they nodded at each other, backing away a little.

The gold shimmer in the air was becoming ever more visible.

Rekka knelt by the prince's case and stroked his light hair. The sun caught in his eyes as he slowly became more lucid, making several attempts to speak before he finally said, in a hoarse whisper,

"Is it over?"

"Yes." said Rekka breathlessly.

"Yes, it's over."

"You stayed the whole time? Like you said? How long was it?" he asked, notes of fear creeping into his voice while he made an attempt to sit up. Rekka helped him, brushing off his clothes even though he had been protected from dust by the case.

"I was here the whole time, the whole long time. Making sure that you were alright." Rekka embraced Hugo, who buried his face in her shoulder.

Edgar looked to Gaia, but she didn't meet his eyes. She was watching Rekka and Hugo intently.

"I forget." she said under her breath. Edgar wasn't sure if she was talking to him or not.

"You... forget what?"

"I forget whether or not I was ever like that. I wrote a lot of it down, but I lost those notebooks. I mean... I was probably attached to people. Before I got tired of outliving them. At what point did I decide that being solitary was better than being sad?"

"I... I wish I could help." Gaia turned her head to Edgar and smiled warmly. She took his hand and the gold in the air intensified and the room grew colder. The room seemed to sway slightly, though maybe it was a trick of the light.

"Maybe there'll be another shot at it on the other side of the disintegration. After all, there's a lot that we don't know about the universe. Even after all this time."

"Yeah. There's a lot."

Outside the snow globe. He thought.

"What's happening?" asked Hugo, his voice muffled against the silk of Rekka's dark blue dress. He peered up, but with one hand Rekka gently pushed his head back down.

"Pay it no heed." Rekka began to rock back and forth, murmuring things that Edgar and Gaia couldn't quite make out. Hugo dug his hands into the fabric. The room began to waver, the air was shining and heavy with gold. The walls were somewhere between melting and turning to sand. Edgar watched, but he had to shut his eyes. He felt like if he looked at it for too long, he would lose his mind.

"You should go. You shouldn't just disappear and leave the people who care about you wondering." said Gaia, her voice sounded at once like it was right in his ear and far away behind a wall of crystal.

"Before it's too late. Go."

Edgar opened his eyes. There were no longer walls. He couldn't comprehend that which had eaten them away. He took one more look at Rekka and Hugo, locked in embrace and rocking back and forth. He looked into Gaia's dark eyes; she nodded. The golden disintegration was to swallow her up. The wind it brought blew her hair about. From all corners of the universe, the shimmering was meeting, and it fought for the last scrap of what existed.

"Goodbye." Edgar disappeared.

Gaia moved to approach Attens-Rekka and Hugo, even though they were in their own little world. It was like walking through deep water though, and the mosaic tiles under her feet did not even exist anymore.

The storm of golden, shimmering, disintegration swallowed up the last tiny bastion, and what lies beyond that nobody can tell.

But so far back in the past was Edgar. He found himself on the sidewalk, near a phone booth. As usual, nobody paid any heed. They were all busy going about their own business.

There was so much. Taxis, cracks in the sidewalk, the distant sounds of people chattering in the pub across the street. So much more than a lonely bed chamber across the stars. He looked up at the gray sky. The universe felt like a much bigger place in the future. In the times of mobile phones, and space travel. The times of colonies on other planets, and opera houses of gold. Eventually though, it would become small again. Just a speck.

To think that someday the entire world would just be Edgar, Gaia, Rekka, and Hugo. What a funny thought.

Right now, everything was far too normal to even imagine something so strange. And yet... Edgar had just witnessed the end of the universe. And now he was on his way to have a pint with his two dear friends. So normal.

It's all a snow globe. He thought, crossing the street.

In a few seconds, Edgar found himself outside that snow globe, as the driver of the bus hurtling down the street had a heart-attack.

He died on the street, and would be remembered for a little while, then forgotten. Forgotten at least, until the very, very end of the universe.

Der Rosenwalzer

1.

"Great job, everyone!" Fiona said, gently resting her cello in its case. "The host gave me the checks, here you guys go!" She passed three checks to us other members of the string quartet.

"Sweet!" said Dante, tucking it into his sheet music folder. "Here's to the happy couple- thanks for making it rain!" he exclaimed.

Emmett relaxed the bow of his viola and nodded in my direction.

"Hey, KT. Good job." he said quietly.

"Thanks Emmett!"

Emmett was rather serious, but he always made a point of telling us all that we'd done a good job whenever we played a gig. It was nice to hear- especially since musicians are notoriously hard on themselves.

"You're welcome. I liked your piano pieces, Dante. Gave us a nice break." Emmett said.

"Thanks! I played Arabesque no.1 by Claude Debussy."

"Yeah, I know." Emmett replied bluntly.

Dante and I both played violin, but I was usually Violin 1 in the quartet, since it wasn't his primary instrument. He was really good at both piano and violin, and had a liking for playing flashy music. It wasn't in his nature to show off to put people down, though. He was just enthusiastic and oblivious at times.

"About ready to go?" Fiona already had her coat on, ready to head out of the hall and into the rain. Typical for April, even in California. Thankfully the wedding party had rented out a hall so we could keep dry.

"I want to play that piano again." Dante sighed, slinging his violin case strap over his shoulder.

"It's such a nice one. Too nice for some random reception hall."

"There's an even nicer one at my home."

I whirled around from buttoning my coat and saw a tall brunette woman. She was incredibly pale- maybe she just looked more so because of her dark blue gown. Her low-cut dress contoured with her like it was custom, and the cut- along with her high heeled shoes- made her both imposing and beautiful. I'm 5'7, and she was at least three inches taller than me. Probably more.

"Sorry, did I scare you? I didn't mean to." she said with a laugh.

"No worries." I said.

"Did you enjoy our playing?" asked Fiona, always ready to talk someone into booking us.

"I did, as a matter of fact." said the woman, extending her hand to Fiona. Fiona shook her hand, and the woman shook all our hands too. "I'm Georgiana Kaplan. Pleasure to meet- and hear- all of you!"

"We're the Eclectic Strings." Fiona said warmly, and introduced us all by name.

Dante and I exchanged glances. I guess Eclectic Strings was what we were going with. Names on the drawing room floor included High Strung Strings, The Four Amigos, and The Whatever Quartet. Coined by Dante, me, and Emmett, respectively.

"I have to say, I'm quite impressed." Ms. Kaplan said. She reached out to take Emmett's folder from him.

"May I see?"

"Um, sure." he said, gingerly handing her his black music folder. It was splitting at the seams a little from the amount of papers inside.

"There's a lot of music in there that we didn't play. This particular gig had a lot of specifically requested music, but we have a lot of string quartet standards and also lesser known pieces in our repertoire!" Fiona explained, as Ms. Kaplan leafed through the pages.

"Impressive repertoire!"

"We're all currently in our undergrad studies at Pacific Conservatory." Fiona continued. Georgiana looked at me and clapped her hands together.

"Lovely, lovely. Now you- I recognize you- weren't you in the Carmel Youth Orchestra?"

"Um… yeah, I was." I said, blushing a little. The name Georgiana Kaplan *was* a little familiar.

"I'm on the donor list- passionate about supporting young artists, you know. I remember KT here- I can't believe that just four years ago she was sitting in the back of the violin section!" she chuckled, and Dante elbowed me playfully.

"If you ask me, if you're fortunate enough to have money you should be spreading it around to help others- right?"

"Mmm hmm." I agreed sheepishly. This woman was partially responsible for the scholarships that made it possible for me to play in the youth orchestra. I realized that I should probably thank her, but I was feeling a little embarrassed about the whole "back of the violin section" remark. I mean, it was true, but still… it wasn't like she had to broadcast that to my college friends.

"So you're pretty involved in local music then? Do you play any instruments?" Dante asked, the keychains on his case jingling as he swayed casually on his feet. I shook my shoulder slightly to make *my* violin case keychains jingle back at him.

"I can navigate a piano pretty well, nowhere near as good a musician as you four. Which brings me to why I came over here in the first place."

Though her face was calm, I could see Fiona's dark brown eyes glistening with excitement. There was a reason she was kind of the face of our quartet.

"My niece is getting married next weekend, on Saturday night. We had a group booked for chamber music but unfortunately they cancelled on us.

Unforeseen circumstances, they said. One of the members broke their arm and they couldn't get a replacement. So as you can imagine, I've been scrambling a little bit, since getting the music was supposed to be my job!" she laughed musically. Fiona nodded her head sympathetically.

"Sounds stressful! I can't imagine."

Dante and I glanced at each other, and his face seemed to say *secure the gig, Fiona!*

"Oh, yes, really stressful. So, what I'm getting at here is- would you four be willing and able to play next Saturday at my niece's wedding?"

Fiona put her tote bag on one of the folding chairs we had been sitting on, and rooted around for a second before pulling out a mini-calendar with daisies on it.

"We have nothing booked for that day- everyone, is this something you can do? Are we all free?"

"Yup." Emmett nodded.

"For sure!" said Dante.

I grinned broadly and had to resist the urge to fist pump. We were trying hard to get consistent gigs that summer, and this felt like the start of something awesome.

"I'd be really happy to."

If we played at this niece's wedding, then all of Ms. Kaplan's rich friends would see us, and want to hire us for their galas and other rich people events!

"Then it's on!" Fiona said, scribbling away in the calendar.

"Now, there is something about this gig. The wedding reception will be starting at 11pm."

Fiona looked up, her eyebrows raising involuntarily.

"PM?" she asked.

"Yes." said Ms. Kaplan, reaching into her purse for her phone.

"11pm. Is that alright?"

"I mean-" Fiona looked at us for any sign of displeasure.

"I mean, yes. I think we're all night owls here."

"Thank you for being so flexible- you can see why it was so difficult to find a replacement! May I have your email?"

"f_skyler2@u.pcom.edu."

"Thank you! I'll send you the details, like call time for sound check and the address of the estate, of course."

"Ooh, *estate*!" exclaimed Dante. "Sounds fancy!"

Ms. Kaplan smiled, revealing splendid white teeth.

"Very. Dinner will be provided for you, of course. Drinks as well, and you will get a break."

"Thank you very much, Ms. Kaplan. Now, our rate is-"

"I was thinking about $700 per player? Would a flat rate like that work for you all?"

My eyes felt like they were going to pop out of my skull, they opened so wide at the sound of that number. I imagined that, like a little cartoon animal, my pupils had turned to dollar signs.

"S-seven hundred?" said Fiona, keeping her composure but clearly surprised in a good way. Usually people were the *opposite-* asking us if we'd be willing to play for *exposure.* As if.

Dante looked at me and mouthed *holy shit!*

"Is that good?" Ms. Kaplan asked.

"Well, of course!" Fiona laughed, and extended her hand. Ms. Kaplan shook it, and the gig was booked.

"I'm looking forward to getting in touch with you once I'm home!"

"We're looking forward to playing for you."

Needless to say, we were all in great spirits as we headed toward Emmett's car to ride home. Even stoic Emmett was cheerful and smiling as he drove us home.

"What music do you think she's going to ask us for?" he mused.

"If it's another Coldplay song, I quit." said Fiona, who had her phone hooked up to the aux cable and was scrolling, taking a little too long to pick a song.

"Maybe we can finally pull out the Ravel!" said Dante.

"Or Philip Glass!" I chimed in.
"People really like Borodin." said Fiona, who was definitely a fan of the Romantic era of music. "She's pretty steeped in classical music, it seems, so I wouldn't be surprised if she asked us for Borodin Quartet no. 2. It's very appropriate for a wedding, Borodin wrote it for his wife."

"So sweet… Do you think Benji would write anything for me?" I said, bunching my sweater up so I could use it as a pillow on the long drive home on the twisty roads of Carmel Valley. I sat back and crossed one leg on top of the other.

"Didn't he dedicate a chord progression he wrote in music theory to you?" Fiona asked, turning around in her seat to talk to me face to face.

"Yeah." I said fondly, fiddling around with a buckle on my shoe. Benji is awesome. Even if he plays the oboe. Just kidding!

"I remember *KT Khords…*" mused Dante, slightly spaced out and staring out the window.

"Can you sit forward, I'm getting nervous." said Emmett, eyes glued to the road and hitting a switch to increase the speed of the windshield wipers, for all the good that did. Fiona sat forward in her seat again.

"It's kind of crazy though. It's almost eleven now, but this time next week we're going to be getting set up." she said.

"Hope there's coffee." said Emmett.

"I don't need coffee to stay up late." said Dante- who immediately proceeded to yawn widely.

"Mmm hmm, really?" I laughed, feeling weight on my own eyelids. I decided to nap in the car, trusting that Emmett wouldn't send us careening off the edge of a cliff.

"These people must be loaded." I heard Dante say while I dozed off.

"Yeah. It's kind of sinister that they can just shell out that much, but honestly? I'm cool with it. What do you want to bet that they're mafia, though?" Fiona said.

"Or maybe they're descended from the Romanovs. Like, they escaped to America and their descendants are filthy rich." suggested Dante.

"Hmmm, that's a good one too. What do you say, KT?"

"Mafia." I muttered before falling asleep to the rhythm of the rain.

2.

It was 10:24, just six minutes to call time, and I was pretty sure we were lost. Not only was it dark, but the rain- which had thankfully let up for a while- had left the roads muddy and dangerous. Carmel Valley was no cakewalk, either. While riding in the backseat of a car rocketing down dark, winding, mountainous roads, getting carsick was the least of my worries.

Emmett reached down to the cupholder and grabbed his travel mug. He took a long sip and put it back down, steering with one hand.

"We're going to be late!" Fiona said mournfully.

"I'd rather not go any faster." Emmett replied. Dante shook his head.

"Nah. Pedal to the metal, Emmett- it's Glory or Death!"

"Are those my *only* options?" Emmett asked though somewhat clenched teeth as he dared to speed up just a touch.

"As a musician, I'd do anything to be on time, but as a passenger I have to say, don't kill us." I said, holding the grab handle above my window for dear life.

"Fiona, what's the next turn?" Emmett asked. Fiona unlocked her phone.

"Hmmm, I've got no signal up here, the map cut out. But…" ever the most prepared out of all of us, Fiona reached down and pulled a folded paper out of her purse- she'd printed the email.

"The email said from here we go right onto Rosewood Drive. Stay on it until the crossroads, you're gonna take a left onto Westenra Boulevard. According to the email, there's a private road that should be open at the moment for us, and that's a right turn. Then we should find the estate."

"Can't get over how fancy that is. *Estate.*" said Dante, pulling on his shoes and tying them in the cramped back seat of Emmett's sedan. For some reason he always took his shoes off in the car. He said it was to prevent scuffing, but I think his dress shoes were just uncomfortable.

The private road was narrow and flanked with heavy forest. Like in *Snow White and The Seven Dwarfs,* the branches were reaching out and smacking the sides of the car as we drove. Emmett sighed, probably thinking about the paint.

"Damn, should really get someone out here to trim back the trees." said Dante. He put his finger on the button to roll down the window and looked at me with his lop-sided grin.

"Dare me?"

"Not unless you want to be reading your music with one eye." I replied.

"The email said we could park right here… not too much of a hike up to the house. I think this is where the guests are parking, too." said Fiona, stopping the car and hopping out.

"I wonder how many people are going to be here?" said Dante, pulling on his jacket as he got out too, and looked around the field behind the house that was serving as a parking lot.

"There's an awful lot of cars." said Fiona.

"Must be a big party, then!" Dante said, his eyes gleaming.

We all trod carefully on the soft, muddy ground, instrument and folders in tow. Occasionally I heard Emmett grunt as he nearly slipped on the mud. We were all happy to finally reach the front of the house- or rather, mansion, and climb up the stairs.

It was probably the fanciest house I had ever been in. It was grand and beautiful, like something out of a Jane Austen book adaptation.

There was a man in a simple yet expensive looking suit standing by the entrance. The guests trickling in showed him their invitations and he checked for them in a guest book he had sitting on a portable podium.

"Do we have the invites?" I asked Fiona, patting my coat pocket to reassure myself that I had the envelope. It was such a pretty invitation, on fancy, ivory colored paper with an almost linen texture, and gold leaf flower decorations, accented with swirling calligraphy in red ink.

"Yeah, I have mine. What about you guys?"

"Yep." said Emmett, pulling it out of his dress pants pocket.

"Shoot. I stuffed mine in my case." Dante slung his violin case off his shoulder, and awkwardly unzipped the side pocket as he walked. A few mechanical pencils spilled out of the side pocket as he fumbled for his invite. I crouched down to grab his pencils.

"Don't worry, I've got 'em."

"Thanks. Aha!" He zipped the pouch shut and held out his mutilated invitation envelope out triumphantly.

"Good god, did you open it with a chainsaw?" I asked.

"Uh, hello." said Fiona to the doorman.

"We're the string quartet, here for the wedding reception."

"Reception? I was informed that you would be playing at the ceremony as well."

"Oh!" said Fiona, a little shadow of alarm passing over her face as her plans were threatened. "Is the ceremony here? We didn't miss it?"

"The ceremony is here, yes. Don't worry, you have plenty of time to set up and make yourselves ready. You'll be shown where to go."

"Alright then." We followed Fiona into the house. I could tell she was confused, but she managed to hide it under a mask of professionalism. If only the rest of us could be so stoic…

"I hope we get paid extra." grumbled Emmett, checking the time on his phone. "A typical wedding ceremony is between an hour to an hour and a half long. The wedding reception could go on for hours. I guess we can kiss getting any sleep goodbye."

"Oh, be quiet, Emmett." hissed Fiona under her breath. "I'll make sure we get paid well for the extra time."

The entryway was gorgeous. There were two staircases that led to an upper level that looked down over the entrance, and there were decorations like statues, fancy rugs, and paintings. It was like Hearst Castle, or the Winchester Mystery House. Under the overhanging part of the second floor was a pair of frosted glass doors that seemed to lead outside to a garden. I wondered if it was appropriate to get pictures for my roommate. For the moment, I resisted the urge to take out my phone and start snapping pictures.

"Oh hello! Are you the musicians?" came a woman's voice. Standing halfway up the stairs was a lady maybe in her thirties, with short, red hair in a pixie cut. Her golden leaf shaped earrings were so long that they almost brushed her bare shoulders.

"Yes. Where should we go for this "ceremony" that the doorman told us about?"

"Right this way." she waved for us and we followed her up the stairs.

"The ceremony is in the Le Fanu Ballroom, and the reception will be down in the Marschner Dining Hall.

"Wow, I've never been in a house where the rooms have actual names." said Dante. The woman laughed, putting a hand over her bright red lips.

"You're so charming!" she said.

"Well, the Kaplan family is very rich. They've been in this area for ages, since before the turn of the century, and while they keep a low-profile they do enjoy the finer things. If Ms. Kaplan herself chose you for the music, you must be incredible! I know she wouldn't settle for anything less."

I blushed. I wasn't even done with undergrad violin studies yet. I was afraid of not living up to expectations, and distracted myself by looking down at the carpet as we walked down this hallway, and up more stairs. As we walked, I saw patterns of dancing skeletons, disembodied heads with bat wings, wyverns with naked ladies riding on their backs torching villages, and other, stranger things that wouldn't look out of place in a Hieronymus Bosch painting. I felt weird walking on it. Especially when we reached the part with a field of impaled heads against a red sky.

"This is an interesting pattern. I haven't seen one like it." Said Fiona.

"Oh, on the carpet? Yes, this is a commission the family had done just for this hallway. It's called *Plagues and Tribulations.*"

"The *rug* has a name, too?!" Dante exclaimed.

"So it's kind of like we're walking on a painting?" Emmett said nervously, trying to step lightly.

"Don't worry about damaging it! It's only out on special occasions, and cleans up just fine."

"I hope so…" Emmett blushed red, sheepishly looking behind him to see if his muddy shoes had left any footprints.

"It's kinda hypnotic." I said, watching the changing of scenes. It wasn't like a series of different pictures, it was like one *long* picture.

"We're here!" said the woman as we reached a wide, open room. On one side was a pair of glass double doors that led to a large, half-circle balcony. The other side of the room was covered in a wide pair of curtains. The woman pulled a thick cord on one side, and the curtains parted to show a pair of ornate double doors. The woman opened one of the doors and gracefully ushered us inside.

"Thank you, um…" said Fiona.

"Camilla Sheridan. Sister of the bride. Also, you'll need this. It's what music to play, when." said the woman, taking a sheet of paper off her clipboard.

"Thank you Ms. Sheridan. This is really helpful. We'll get set up."

We walked in, and saw around fifteen rows of folding chairs lined up before a fancy archway with a podium underneath. All were decorated with roses. There weren't any windows except for a skylight. The walls were covered in sweeping, red velvet curtains.

"I guess that's us?" I said, looking to the back corner of the room and noticing four folding chairs with four music stands.

"I see Ms. Kaplan up there at the podium thing. I'm going to ask what we should play and *when* we should play it."

"Right." said Emmett, sitting down and getting his viola out.

"They, there's a piano near the front. I wonder if they want any piano music, too. Do you think that's the piano Kaplan was talking about back when she hired us?"

"Maybe." I said, applying rosin to my bow.

"Dante, before you go play chopsticks, we have to rehearse a few spots. Get used to the acoustics and set up. According to this list, we're supposed to play the Borodin Nocturne on the maid of honor's signal. That'll let the guests know the wedding is starting soon, they can all get to their seats and quiet down."

"I knew it!" I said. "I knew they couldn't resist the Nocturne."

"I know, right? So, we're supposed to play all the way through- then immediately start Air on the G string, Bach."

"We know it's Bach, Fiona." said Emmett, nervously bouncing his leg and propping his viola up on his knee.

"Then," she said, ignoring him, "after the officiant says that they're husband and wife, we start this next piece- *Der Rosenwalzer.*"

I dug around in my folder, rearranging the pieces in the order we'd play them in. I hadn't heard of *Der Rosenwalzer* before, and we couldn't find sheet music for it anywhere. That didn't matter though,

because Ms. Kaplan sent it to us, saying it wasn't in
the public domain or anything because it was an old,
old waltz that somebody in the family had composed
but never published. I liked the program notes,
scribbled in German along the top of the score.
Thank you, translator app on my phone.

A waltz to soothe the aching appetites of my family.

So weird! I found myself consumed by
curiosity. I myself had an *aching appetite* for whatever
the meaning of that was.

Anyway!

Practicing a piece you can't find a recording of
is interesting, because you don't know what it's going
to sound like until you play it with the others. I have
to say, I really liked it, and I scanned all the parts into
my phone. I did it when the others weren't looking. I
didn't need Fiona going to Ms. Kaplan and
mentioning I had done so- there was a note with the
mailed parts that said for us to *not* scan it, because it
was a cherished family secret, yada-yada-yada.

But I have a weakness for secrets, lost stories,
and music that charms my imagination. I couldn't
help myself.

Besides, if she never finds out, what's the
harm? It's for my own personal enjoyment. That's
what I told myself.

3.

We didn't run through anything all the way through. On concert days, we saved our energy for the *actual* thing. We touched up on a few spots, tuned to each other a few times as we warmed up, and then just sat there waiting. Dante couldn't sit still- as was usual before a gig- and was holding his violin like it was a guitar, plucking out his part of the Ravel. The second movement of the Ravel was fun. We were saving that for the reception. I countered by plucking part of the Philip Glass- string quartet no. 5- and Dante started plucking the Ravel louder.

"Dante, come on." said Fiona. "Gotta look professional."

"More like, gotta look *enthusiastic!*" he replied. "That's how you get more gigs- people don't say, wow I want to hire that *professional* looking musician, they say wow I loved that *enthusiastic* musician."

"No, Dante, I'm pretty sure we get hired for being professional. Being on time, and knowing our parts."

"Hopefully we know our parts then, because we weren't really on time." mumbled Emmett.

More people were filing into the ballroom. A lot of them had glasses of wine already, so there must've been some kind of pre-wedding party. A lot of them didn't sit down right away- they immediately flocked to their friends, crying out in delight at faces they hadn't seen in ages, apparently. The buzz of indistinct voices and conversation filled the room, and it reminded me of a movie theater before the trailers started.

"Let's tune again." Fiona mouthed. I nodded, and started playing my A. The others joined in, once I had found it (and the little green light on my tuner was nice and steady). The sound of instruments tuning together always grounded me before a performance, and a lot of my nervous energy evaporated.

Fiona's timing was right on the money. We saw the sister of the bride nod at us from the decorated archway at the front of the room.

Dante, Emmett, and Fiona got their instruments up and ready, while I just stayed in rest position. I didn't come in right away at the beginning. Dante breathed, and he and Emmett started playing a syncopated pattern that Fiona wove a sweet and delicate melody over. The three of them sounded so beautiful together, sending a calm but firm signal to the room that it was time to be quiet and sit down. I almost didn't come in on time, but I had listened to and played the piece so often that knowing when I came in was automatic.

That high note entrance used to scare me. It's so vulnerable to make an entrance on a high note marked *piano*, but now instead of thinking *wow it's so high! And it has to be quiet!*, I thought to myself *wow, I love playing this melody*. Somehow that made it easier to come in, quiet and in tune.

4.

I've played at a lot of weddings, and heard a lot of different variations on the traditional vows. I once went to a wedding where the bride and groom unironically had "you're the peanut butter to my jelly" as part of it. That still wasn't as odd as this one.

The bride walked down the aisle herself, up to the archway where the officiant and the groom were waiting. Like a regular wedding, the bride and groom stood, hands folded together in front of the officiant. The officiant was actually *Ms. Kaplan*, which I know *I* wasn't expecting. I remember thinking, *is she a protestant minister?* She wasn't wearing anything that looked particularly protestant, or even ceremonial. She was just wearing a simple black gown, once again cut to amplify her height.

The bride and groom had their vows memorized, and recited them after Mrs. Kaplan read from a burgundy, leatherbound book. The reading didn't *sound* biblical, or like any religion's holy book I'd heard of before, but it did sound like the kind of thing a minister would read at a wedding. Stuff about love, faithfulness, how once you are family, you are bound by blood forever no matter what. It was a little aggressive and on the nose, but overall the sentiment was nice, I guess.

Truth be told, I sort of spaced out during the ceremony. It wasn't until I saw Fiona (eyes like a hawk, that one) pick up her cello and put it into playing position. She nodded at us and I saw Dante make a mad scramble to put his sheet music in the right order. He was fidgeting around with it during the ceremony because he got bored.

This was my third time hearing the piece all the way through. The first time I heard it during rehearsal, it took my breath away just from how *cool* it was. Flouncy and mischievous, angular yet graceful, moody yet cheerful, a bouquet of contradictions that somehow got along. Words don't do it justice. My phone was recording it in my pocket, and every so often I listen to it, just to see if it's still as good as I remember. It truly is a shame that this composer is completely unknown.

5.

The Marschner Dining Hall was gorgeous. There were small chandeliers spaced across the ceiling, as well as swooping cloth banners gently swaying in the circulating air. The bride and groom were seated with immediate family at a table at the end of the room, facing at least two dozen small, circular tables and a large open section of floor for dancing. We were up toward the big table, four chairs and music stands all set up for us. According to our itinerary, we were going to play a little bit of music while people were served and ate, then after the first dance, we were allowed to go up and get some food during our break.

"Wow, waiters?" Emmett mumbled. "I hate weddings with waiters, what's wrong with getting up off your rich ass and getting your own food?"

"I dunno." I said, sitting down and putting rosin on my bow.

"What do you think they're having?" Dante asked, craning his pale neck.

"Guys, they want music while the food's coming out." Fiona's bow was already on the string.

"Let's do Mozart *Dissonance*, first movement. C'mon, c'mon, wake up."

We have this one memorized, so no awkward shuffling of papers was necessary. I did question Fiona's choice of piece for this particular occasion, though. Mozart's String Quartet no. 19, nicknamed "Dissonance", is beautiful, and probably one of his most famous quartets, but the intro is kind of angsty and ominous sounding before it gets all bouncy and elegant. However, we knew that Ms. Kaplan was a lover of classical music, and I realized that Fiona was just serving them up more austere stuff just because she knew they'd recognize it. Sure enough, at one point, my eyes wandered over to the big table and I made eye contact with Ms. Kaplan, and she shot me a wink.

For the bride and groom's dance, we played *Der Rosenwalzer* again, and then we played the third movement of the Borodin.

The reception of our performance was warm, and Fiona even made us play a short encore. It was a minuet and trio from a Haydn quartet, the encore we always pull out when people clap for a really long time.

When we finished the Haydn, Fiona looked back at Ms. Kaplan to confirm that we could go on break. She nodded, and then Fiona turned and nodded at us as if we didn't also see Ms. Kaplan.

"Disperse!" Fiona said, lying her cello in its case.

As we walked across the hall to the refreshment table that was apparently just for us, I heard cheerful piano music playing over speakers as the other guests gradually got up to join in the dancing.

I chanced a look at a table as we passed by and saw that everyone had the same entree of rare steak with some vegetables, as well as a glass of wine. I realized that there weren't any kids at this wedding. Not too unusual for an event in this area, but it *was* kind of weird that at a big family event there were no kids.

The refreshment table had salmon, mashed potatoes, buns, and assorted vegetables. There were also glasses next to pitchers of lemonade, water, and punch. As I was assembling my plate, Camilla Sheridan approached us from behind.

"You are free to eat at that table over there, and the nearest restrooms are out and down the hall to your left. You all sound lovely, by the way!" she patted me and Dante on the shoulder before she slipped back to the main table.

That was good to know, I was planning on excusing myself to the bathroom and exploring the mansion a bit while I was out. I mean, what's the point of having a gig in a huge mansion if you're not going to take advantage of it a little? I don't mean stealing or anything, I just wanted some pictures of that cool carpet from earlier.

"Whoa, it's 12:01, guys." said Dante in a low voice. "It's officially tomorrow."

"No, it's officially today." I said back.

"I wonder why they had it so late." Emmett thought out loud. "I mean, I get it. If I was super rich,

I would want to just do crazy things just because I could.”

“Yeah, it probably doesn’t go deeper than that.” said Fiona. “We’re getting a major paycheck from this, so I say they’re just bored rich people who wanted to be different. Besides, they seem nice.”

“KT. You wanna rate the dancers?” Dante asked, leaning forward on the table. We play this game at every wedding gig. I don’t really know my dance names, but whatever they were all doing looked kind of coordinated. I wasn’t surprised that they all knew old timey dance steps, given how fancy they were.

“Sure.” I replied. “What do you think of the bride? I’d say a solid 9/10, she’s a little stiff but technically good.”

“Oh yeah. The groom, he looks like a 6/10, y’think? He looks like he’s struggling a bit to keep up with the others. But he’s got the right idea. Gotta say, dude looks thrilled.”

The game wasn’t nearly as fun that time. Everyone was too good. It was like they actually practiced or something. It was actually kind of cool to watch, and eventually we just started all chatting quietly while watching.

Then, Ms. Camilla tapped Dante on the back.

“Oh, hi.” he said in his typically friendly manner.

“Hello! You’re the one who likes to play piano, right? Would you like to take a look at the piano in the library?” she said, leaning over with her hand on his shoulder. I glanced at Fiona and Emmett to see if they noticed the way her fingers gently brushed his shoulder, but Emmett was reading a book he brought, and Fiona was busy eating and answering a text message.

"Oh! Sure." Dante said in response to Ms. Camilla. I wanted to follow them, but I also wanted to explore by myself.

"How come he gets to play the piano?" Emmett asked, looking up. Camilla had spirited him away so quickly the rest of us couldn't get a word in edgewise. Fiona shrugged and made a non-committal face.

"He's the one who made a big deal about the piano at the last gig." She went back to browsing on her phone while eating mashed potatoes on autopilot.

I stood up and pushed my chair back against the table.

"Whelp, I'm gonna go use the bathroom. Don't wait up."

"We're due back on in fifteen minutes." Fiona said without looking away from her phone.

"I never take that long." she was probably onto me. "Besides, even the bride and groom left for a second."

"Gross, and while their guests are still here." said Emmett. I gave him a courtesy laugh and left.

It was much quieter out in the hallway. I decided to look back upstairs, past the wedding room. That would take me over the cool rug I wanted pictures of. I got a notification on my phone, but before I could read it, I instinctively swiped it out of the way to get more pictures.

My footsteps were the only thing that cut through the stillness, thumping loudly on the wooden stairs.

"Yes." I whispered to myself as I turned on the second-floor hallway and saw the long rug. I took out my phone and started taking pictures as I walked.

Where's Dante, anyway?

I started pressing my ear against various doors, listening for piano music. It was sort of chilly on the second story, and I got goosebumps on my arms. Looking up, I noticed that the small windows lining the top of the wall were cracked open. I sort of regretted wearing the sleeveless dress. Why did I leave my cardigan draped over my chair back in the dining room?

As I was rubbing my arms in an attempt to warm up-

-Dear GOD I can see my breath! -

- I heard faint piano music from down the hall a ways. It sounded like one of the pieces in Dante's rotation.

"Alrighty!" I started to lightly jog down the hall, and eventually broke into a run. What is it about long hallways that make me want to sprint?

As I ran though, the piano music abruptly stopped. I was able to tell what room it was coming from though, because I soon came across a set of ajar double doors. There was low light slipping through the gap and into the hallway. I peered between the doors, ready to playfully say *here's Johnny*, but there wasn't anyone there.

I let myself into the lounge, taking in the full bookshelves and nine foot grand piano. It was a really nice room, complete with a big, curtained off window. I could only imagine how good the lighting was during the day. I thought to myself, *if I ever am in desperate need of a place to film my jury, I'll be sure to ask Ms. Kaplan.*

"Dante?" I asked, like a stupid bimbo in a horror movie. Looking at the piano bench, I noticed that it was pushed back, like somebody had just been sitting on it and didn't put it back under the keyboard.

"Hello?" I looked around. It sure was dim. There was another door though, just across the room. They could've gone through there.

The nine foot grand *was* gorgeous, though, and I just *had* to sit down-

-Well, I guess I don't HAVE to sit down-

-and try playing some of my pieces out. All music majors, regardless of instrument concentration, have to take a few semesters of piano, and I was actually getting pretty good. Not like I was that impressive next to Dante, but as long as he wasn't around to innocently show me up...

The touch on Ms. Kaplan's piano was heavenly, the sound was like liquid, and controlling the dynamics was so easy! It made me feel like I was some amazing pianist giving a solo recital at Carnegie Hall. I can just see myself on the front cover of the program... It was almost hypnotic! Maybe it *was* hypnotic, because I didn't notice that Emmett had come in until he smacked the top of the keyboard, playing a cluster of high notes.

"Ah!" I cried out, turning around. "Jeez, Emmett, you *scared* me!"

Emmett blinked slowly, the way he did when he was trying very hard not to roll his eyes.

"We have to go tune. Where's Dante?"

"I thought he was in here, what with the big-ass piano and stuff. But he's not, I couldn't find him."

Emmett pursed his lips and folded his arms, eyes scanning the room.

"He *knew* we didn't have an infinite amount of time to just hang around, right? Didn't he know how long our break was?"

I shrugged, making a face.

"I don't think Dante thinks that far ahead. If it's not right in front of his face-"

"-it might as well not exist, yeah. Outta sight, outta mind, we can get that engraved on his tombstone when he inevitably walks himself off of a cliff because he was too distracted chasing butterflies or something."

"Wow, feeling kind of saucy today, aren't you?" I said, getting up off the bench and following Emmett to the other door in the library.

"I'd just like it if for *once* we weren't all holding our breath waiting for him, that's all. But no. I mean, I don't really give a crap about being the most professional quartet on the planet, but it would be nice if our paychecks weren't in jeopardy." said

Emmet, cautiously twisting the doorknob and slowly cracking the door open, as if worried that we'd get caught, like naughty little children on Christmas Eve.

This other room was dark- the only light was some scant moonlight from the windows and a sliver of yellow lighting from another door that hung slightly open. We became aware of the sound of other people from this other room beyond the lounge we were peering into.

"That sounds like-"

Emmett put his finger to his mouth and gave me a very effective *shut up* look. The noises were soft, but I swear, they sounded like, well, sex. Nothing weird about that, seeing as there was a wedding reception going on and all. Isn't that some old joke or stereotype? No, the weird- read: hilarious- part was that I recognized that voice. It was Dante. I put my hand over my mouth and the urge to laugh was overpowering. I had no idea he would go at it so easily with some rando at a wedding- I knew him well and it didn't seem like he would do that. Honestly, Fiona would be *livid* if she ever found out, because it seems like one of the least professional things you can possibly do at a gig. I started to tiptoe into the dark room, both hands clapped over my mouth as the occasional burst of air from my mouth escaped. Emmett kept whispering, *hey, hey, stop*, but I didn't pay any attention to him. I don't know what I was thinking I would do. I guess I thought that making a loud noise to scare them would be hilarious.

I was going to knock on the door-

-I'm not going to look, *that would be creepy and weird!-*

-and jump scare them, but as I raised my hand, I heard a shift in the noises. The woman was louder, despite being somewhat muffled, and Dante sounded like he was in *pain.*

"S-stop…"

My breath caught in my throat at a *wet, slurping* sound, and I looked through the door. I think Emmett heard it too, because in a moment he was breathing in my ear, one hand on my shoulder as he looked over me.

We saw Dante and that Camilla lady on top of him. Her dress was hiked up around her thighs, and his shirt was unbuttoned with his jacket nowhere to be seen. She had her face buried in his neck, kissing it, pinning both his wrists down. He was weakly struggling, and his pinned down hands were twitching. Dante's head was tilted in our direction, eyes wide and bugged out, but he wasn't looking at us, he was looking *through* us, even as he moaned in pain.

Emmett grabbed my wrist, but I still burst through the door.

"Hey! What's going on in here!?" I can't believe that I did this, but I grabbed Camilla by the back of her dress and threw her off of Dante.

When I did, a chunk of his neck ripped out in her teeth, and blood spurted out of his neck. I jumped back and screamed, I think Emmett did too, and Camilla was left stunned on the floor, on her back propping herself upright with her arms.

"Holy Shit!" I fall to my knees and try to stifle the blood with the hem of my dress. "Dante, Dante, are you okay?" I pressed the material as far into the wound as I could, but his face was drained of color, and only getting worse. "Emmett, help!"

Emmett was too busy confronting Camilla. She'd risen to her feet, licking her lips and *chewing*. She put her hand over her mouth, and stretched the other one out as Emmett stood between her and us.

"Stay back, stay away from us!"

Camilla swallowed - Emmett told me this later, I was still too busy trying to help Dante - and stammered, but couldn't get any words out.

I looked up from Dante when I heard another voice. Ms. Kaplan had thrown the door open and flicked the light switch on, hands on her hips as if walking in on a little kid touching an antique vase. Fiona was with her, dashing over to Dante and tripping on her high heels. She fell and must've gotten carpet burns on her knees.

"Oh my god! What the - what *happened* here?" Fiona said, somewhat incoherently, as Ms. Kaplan calmly walked past Emmett and grabbed both of Camilla's hands, grasping them behind the latter's back and walking her out of the room.

"Keep the pressure on it, I'll be right back." she said, about to shut the door.

"What's happening?" I asked, tears finally breaking free and streaming down my face. I felt my hands shaking, and I doubted my ability to keep enough pressure on the wound. Fiona got up and yanked a doily off a little coffee table, sending the vase under it crashing down onto the floor. The doily was quickly dyed scarlet, and as the world came back into focus I felt hot, sticky blood on my fingers, and heard Dante's ragged breathing as it started to slow. I didn't know if that was good or bad, was he starting to die, or was he calming down?

I don't know ANYTHING about this stuff! I'm a violinist! I didn't expect this kind of shit at my fucking GIG. I just wanted money for playing music and now Dante is going to die!

"Guys… guys, what the hell happened?" Fiona asked breathlessly. Without waiting for an answer, she spoke again. "Emmett. Emmett, call 911." Emmett had been standing stock still with his back to us, but he reacted fast and reached into his pocket, dialing the number without saying a word.

We could hear the phone trying to make the call, but my heart sank even further when it disconnected, and Emmett dialed again.

"No signal. I hate Carmel." he said. "What, are we too goddamn rich for fucking CELL TOWERS?" he said, his voice making a gradual crescendo as he tried again, and again to get the call through.

Ms. Kaplan returned through the same door she left and locked it behind her. She was alone and somber, a wad of gauze pads and bandages in her hand.

"May I?" she knelt next to our friend, gesturing for us to move our hands away. As soon as the pressure was released, more blood churned out of the ragged wound in his throat, but she almost instantly clapped a square of gauze over it. Then another, as blood soaked through the first one. She heaped on all five of the gauze pads she had been carrying, then gently lifted his head so she could wind the bandage around his throat to secure the bandages. The sides and back of his head were soaked, I realized that he'd been lying in a growing pool of his own blood, his hair stained with the stuff.

"Ms. Kaplan-" Fiona spoke first. I could see her trying not to look at her hands, or the crimson lace doily crumpled up in them.

"Camilla is thirty-one, but she lives here with me." Ms. Kaplan said quickly and quietly. "She doesn't have a job, and she can't go out without me or her sister going with her. There's something very wrong with her, she can't-" she took a deep breath and shut her eyes, grimacing. "She can't control herself. She's got these urges, and she can't control them. Even drugged up and seeing a therapist, she's just... not able to control herself. I actually... I actually feel sorry for her. I understand though, if you just hate her. Do try and understand how painful existence is for somebody like that. I really thought that tonight, she would be able to behave herself. I *truly* did, especially with the rest of our family here to keep an eye on her. If I had known that something like this was even a risk - I wouldn't have - I wouldn't have... you wouldn't even be here." she said in a strained voice, biting her lips every time she paused. I noticed her fists were clenched tightly.

"We have to call an ambulance," said Fiona. "Emmett, keep trying-"

"I'll have someone drive you all. We've had to call an ambulance before, for Camilla, and they ended up getting hopelessly lost. Please, it's the least I can do. Let one of us drive your friend to Carmel Valley Hospital, and we'll just say that… we'll say it was a wild animal or something. Please. I can't have Camilla arrested again, the authorities, they don't understand. They see someone like her, and they just want to lock her up where she'll hurt herself or be mistreated."

Her previous air of refined professionalism was gone. I realized then, the reason for this wedding late in the dead of night. They couldn't risk Camilla getting out, could they? Not in a busy tourist city like Carmel. Why not have it late at night? Even if she did get out, it was so dark and wet outside that she wouldn't get far. I understood everything perfectly, or at least I *thought* that I did. That didn't change anything. It didn't change my sudden hatred of Ms. Kaplan and her stupid family.

"You really think that being holed up in this house is best for her?" Fiona said in a shaking voice. "You'd really deny your niece the psychiatric care she obviously *needs*? This isn't just your family, this is our friend! He could die-"

"He won't die." said Ms. Kaplan, putting one of Dante's arms around her neck and standing up, pulling him up off the ground with her. His head flopped lifelessly onto his chest. "Help me take him down to the foyer. I'll make sure the guests don't see anything. You'll also be more than compensated for- for what happened tonight. I'm sure you don't want to wait around for me to write a check, you'll get it in the mail." she said, nodding in thanks at Emmett as he helped her with Dante.

Fiona jumped up suddenly and held the door for them, leaving me alone, kneeling on the floor.

6.

Dante was stretched out across the back seat of this fancy car, I think it was a Lamborghini. Ms. Kaplan's doorman was filled in on everything that happened, and barely even said anything as she explained in hushed tones what Camilla had done.

I realized how short Dante was, especially as Emmett, in all his 6'2 glory, helped secure him in the back seat.

"I'll ride with the doorman, and Emmett, KT, you guys go home. I'll take care of everything." Fiona said wearily. "Please make sure all our instruments and stuff get loaded up into your car."

Emmett nodded, his face still frozen in a blank, slight frown. He didn't make eye contact, he kept staring out into space.

Around twenty minutes later, me and Emmett were in his car, driving off the estate. Though we tried to grab everything- awkwardly walking through the reception room, still full of cheerful people - I shivered and realized that I forgot my cardigan.

Emmett must've noticed that I was cold, because he turned the heater up.

"Do you think Fiona's going to call the cops? Even after Ms. Kaplan explained everything?" I asked, after several attempts to clear my throat.

"I don't know. I hope so. She probably will." said Emmett. "I know that Ms. Kaplan doesn't want her niece to get in trouble, but… so far as I'm concerned, the one at fault here is that bitch. She knew it was a danger, but she wanted her fancy party anyway."

"… yeah." We hit a bump as it started to pour again.

"I guess you're going to have quite a bit to catch Benji up on, huh. You should, I dunno, text him or something. Let him know something happened." he said after he switched on the windshield wipers to a higher setting. It was reassuring and odd to hear Emmett offer such thoughtful advice.

"Ditto you and Aiko." I said. "She'll never let you take a gig again." I wondered if it was appropriate to joke, especially when we weren't even 100% sure Dante would be okay. But I figure now, that was the only way I knew how to cope without crying.

"At least I'm not the one who got… got my throat bitten out." He said distantly.

The way he said it made it seem like he hadn't actually processed it until just now when he spoke the words.

Throat. Bitten. Out.

That's the kind of thing you never expect to see in your life. Horror movies, yes, nightmares, yes, but real life?

The heater was blasting, though I still was cold all the way home.

7.

It's been a week since Dante was released from the hospital. Fiona did call the cops, and told the doctors that it was a human bite, but there wasn't any way to make anything happen. They did a welfare check on the house, but they couldn't find it. That's unbelievable, right? They couldn't find it.

Me, Fiona, and Benji went driving, just to see if *we* could find it, but we couldn't. Even following the directions from the email, it's like the mansion had vanished from the face of the earth. It wasn't even anywhere online.

The hospital says that there's no infection, but Dante is sick. We ask him what he remembers, and he says he remembers nothing after the piano. He says it's all a blur, like he was hypnotized. His fever is staying high, and he can barely eat without throwing it up. The doctors just say to make sure he gets fluids. The wound on his neck is still hurting him and it looks awful, but the doctors insist there's no infection, it's just discoloration. I know, I know, I'm not a doctor. But something is very wrong.

I feel crazy the first time I do it, but I do some research. Just typing in simple, bare-bones phrases at first. The idea in the back of my head is silly. So stupid that I don't even share it with the others.

Over the past few days I have become more and more sure that I know what the problem is.

A wedding late at night.

Strange, oddly violent vows.

A family where the young aunt is revered as a matriarch and obeyed without question.

Bloody, almost uncooked steaks.

A woman driven mad with bloodlust, tearing at human flesh and devouring it.

A waltz, surely meant to soothe and dim those monstrous appetites.

The fact that Ms. Kaplan licked Dante's blood off her finger when she thought nobody was looking.

I need to find somebody who can help Dante, because I believe in my heart that he has been bitten by a vampire.

Bones in the Forest

I almost told her the first time I met her. Well, that's one of two things I almost did. The other thing was leaving and never calling the number she gave me. A national park gift shop- what a funny place to meet someone. I was just buying a map, a much better and more detailed one than what you get at the front gate. She liked my T-shirt - it had the logo of an obscure 90s comedy show on it, and she recognized it. She asked me my favorite episode. I told her. She liked that one too. I learned her name, it was Rachel.

"Too bad you're probably from really far away or something."

"Actually I'm from Mariposa." that was just under an hour away, the closest town.

"Wow! No kidding, huh." I saw her eyes light up. I looked around to see if anyone was in line behind me, worried I was holding up a line or something, but nobody was behind me. She kept talking.

"My lunch break is soon. Do you wanna eat at one of those benches outside?"

I had lunch packed, I shrugged and said I'd go get it from my car and meet her there.

I don't know why I agreed. I think I was just happy to meet someone who recognized my shirt. It was the only show I really liked to watch, after all.

We ate lunch together, in the midsummer heat, and I actually found myself compelled to talk more than I had ever felt compelled to talk with another person. I caught myself staring at her blue jay pendant, but always pulled my focus away from that and looked at her face instead, as hard as it was for me.

***

Sitting in a small restaurant at noon, waiting on two orders of fettuccine alfredo, me and Rachel were both checking our emails on our phones. People passing by probably were shaking their heads, thinking things like "couples these days don't even look at each other."

Preemptively, I was annoyed. I thought to myself, shut up all of you. Rachel and I had spent all of last night wrapped up in each other. I think we're allowed to check out goddamn phones while waiting for lunch.

"Christian." she said, bringing me back down to earth. She held her phone up to me. It was a meme. An ornithology meme. I chuckled convincingly, and she smiled. I always tried to laugh at her ornithology memes.

Not even her fellow conservation-nature-national park people really got them. So it was the least I could do.

But acting was hard that day.
***

"You've made so much progress, are you proud?" she said, from her cushioned chair, notebook balanced on her crossed, nylon legs.

I was sitting on the couch in her office. Sometimes I got distracted by the mini fountain on her desk. What if she elbowed it and the water went all over the keyboard? Would it break?

"Christian." she said again. I'd spaced out, thinking about that mini fountain.

"I'm happy with my progress." I said, basically repeating back what she had asked me.

"That's good. That's good. Your mom was telling me that you seem so much better than last year." she paused. "How would you feel going from weekly to biweekly? I think that if you feel ready, then that's a good transition to make."

I shrugged.

"Sure. I'm okay with that." and I put a smile on my face. I was okay with seeing Arlene fewer times. I was fourteen. I both craved and hated being alone with the young, inexperienced therapist covered by my mom's modest insurance plan.

I sometimes couldn't stop myself from looking up her pinstripe skirt when she uncrossed and recrossed her legs. She didn't know it, but I internally sighed in relief when she wore pants instead. I was also secretly a little disappointed.

There was enough going on in my brain that made me uneasy, and I didn't want to add hiding my lap from my thirty-four year old therapist on top of all that.

    ***

The two orders of pasta arrived, just a few minutes before the time Rachel had appointed as the time she would go and inquire at the front counter.

She dug in right away and spent a few more minutes looking at her phone. Sometimes she glanced up at me sheepishly smiling. I returned the smile. I didn't really eat much of it. I'd probably end up taking all this home in a takeout box.

Usually, this was when Rachel would ask me, *why aren't you eating?*, but today she just kept smiling sheepishly. Maybe it was because of what happened last night. We were quiet, but it wasn't for the usual reasons people close to each other stopped talking. Far from it. What happened last night was so unexpected, and even though it was supposedly a good thing, it had left us without any words. Maybe because we had just expressed everything we needed to without words.

It wasn't planned, it just happened. On my living room floor, after a night spent watching our favorite show for hours, nothing outside the window except the black void of the night time streets and their yellow, artificial stars.

    ***

An awkward car drive, about an hour and a half long. No music played as we drove to Arlene's office for the first time. I tried not to be upset that my mom barely spoke to me. I knew she was trying her best. There was no getting around it though, no getting around the signs she kept saying she was hating herself for missing. Blood under my fingernails, three pocket knives she didn't even know I had showing up in the laundry somehow, and then the big one. An old, metal toolbox that she hadn't been meant to find, in a corner of the backyard I had never thought she would try to turn into a vegetable garden.

I remembered the day, a week ago just about, that I found her sitting in the kitchen when I came home from school, the box on the table. I'd wanted to just run away. I thought she was going to kill me or something, but she just stared me dead in the eye and asked question after question in a low voice.

***

Wandering through the aisles of the antique shop Rachel and I walked into, I was reminded of my grandma's house. There were so many odd little figurines; one of a pig in a gingham dress at a butter churn, another one of a china angel with big, pleading eyes- there were a lot of angels- and another one that caught my eye was a seated Snow White, with a little blue bird perched on her finger.

"I wanna get out of this section." said Rachel, peering out at me from behind the shelves. "I feel like I'm gonna accidentally knock something down and start a domino effect."

I nodded.

"Sure."

"They have 99¢ books over there, they're super beat up, but if there's anything good I'm snatching it up, and I don't care if there's mysterious stains on the title page."

"Sure." I chuckled distantly.

"You've got like, a huge pile of books that you haven't even touched." she said, moving to the shelves stocked with ratty old books, and running her finger across the bottom of the shelf as she read the titles.

"Yeah. No harm in adding a few more though." I leaned over her shoulder. They were mostly old romance novels and some classics. I picked up a copy of *Medicine for Melancholy*, one that looked like it was about to disintegrate, but I still figured I'd pick it up. I'd always wanted to read that one. I had the author's other short story collections, so this one completed the collection.

Eventually, I'd get around to reading the rest.

Rachel on the other hand, was on the lookout for something different. The absolute trashiest, smuttiest, shameless romance novels- that's what she was looking for.

Not like Rachel was into that kind of thing seriously, but she found them hilarious, and if she could get them for less than five bucks, she'd pick them up. It had started in college, she said. She and her classmates were always assigned huge chunks of their biology textbooks, and so as a sort of relief, they went to the thrift store near campus and bought the worst books they could find.

"This one looks pretty porn-tastic." said Rachel, leafing through the yellow pages of a book titled *Chained to an Adonis*. She looked around. "Aw damn, there's an old lady nearby, otherwise I'd treat you to a reading."

"I guess that'll have to wait." I said, about to put my arm around her shoulder, but then for some reason I didn't, and my hand stayed at my side, sweating and making me feel like I was going to dissolve the frail cover of my book.

"You wanna get going?" I asked.

"C'mon, just a little while longer. I want to look at the clothes people died in."
***

The biggest thing I ever killed was a raccoon. I was riding my bike home from school, down a stony backroad that cut through the woods when I found it. Some car, maybe a service truck or something, had hit it, but it was still alive. I stopped my bike and squatted down for a closer look. My little knife was heavy in my pants pocket. The little thing was squirming in pain, making awful little noises. Its leg was hanging on by just a tendon. I wondered if it would survive if I just left it. My grandpa would probably kill it quickly with a shovel or something, my mom would've just left it. I'm not sure what my dad would've done. Probably shake his head and say that it was too bad, but that's the kind of stuff you signed up for when you lived in a remote, rural town.

I went off the path a bit, so that on the off chance a car passed by, the driver wouldn't see me. There was a lot I did with my animals, but it was never out of malice. I think people don't realize that, they don't even take the time to consider it. I might've played with it a little, but it wasn't because I wanted the raccoon to hurt. Arlene would help me figure it out a few years later, but I think it was more of a morbid curiosity thing, as opposed to anything sinister.

Still, I can see how carefully cutting off the head of a raccoon and skinning it so I could keep the skull would be a little sinister to some people. That's why I did it in secret though, and that's why nobody knew outside of Arlene and close family.

***

"What should we do next free weekend?" Rachel asked me, checking her work schedule on the phone as we left the antique shop. The park service usually had her working on weekends- lots of tourists coming up, especially now that it was summertime- but in two weeks she had another free weekend like this one.

"Do we have to plan something? We could just wing it. We're winging it today, and it's really nice."

"Yeah, well, next week I want to drive somewhere. Somewhere kinda far away. Like… the Winchester Mystery House or something! It's only around three hours away from here, so we can make it a day trip, and do more than just the house. Nice dinner somewhere, find another bookstore to browse… go to a huge mall and check out all the stores they don't have around here, y'know, big city stuff."

I hit the crosswalk button and we waited.

"I like the sound of the mystery house."

"Have you ever been?"

"No."

"I have, a really long time ago when I was a kid. My fourth grade class went."

The little blinking *walk* letters flashed and we kept talking as we crossed the street.

"Sounds like you went all kinds of places for field trips as a kid."

"Well, schools in the bay area have no shortage of places to ship the kids off to. The Winchester House was my favorite, though, aside from the Yosemite trip of course. I love the spooky stuff. Ghosts, murder, people going crazy, I felt like I was visiting a cool book or movie!"

"Yeah." I said distantly.

"I kinda get that vibe from this town. I feel like there's something cool going on under the surface or something. A town this small, gotta be something going on. You grew up here, did you ever have anything eerie?" she asked, eyes gleaming with curiosity. I couldn't help but smile, it was so charming to me when she smiled like that.

"Well, I dunno. Normal gossip stuff, who's seeing who, so-and-so stopped going to so-and-so's diner, this tourist or that tourist fell off Vernal Falls, what a shame…" I paused. "There was this one interesting story, when I was in middle school."

"Oh really?"

***

"Mountain lions don't just take the heads." Alice had said in the hallway between math and english. She was at her locker, talking with Hannah and Hannah's twin brother George.

I slowed down to listen to them. I didn't typically hang out with Alice or her crowd, or anyone, really, so walking slowly down the hallway was the best way to catch all the news.

"What about the birds? The wings are gone too, according to you, anyway. It's possible something was just eating them." said George.

"But it looks too neat. I think somebody's doing it for a reason. Something like a *cult*."

The cult rumor spread like crazy through the school. People were always talking about it, and the thing is, that didn't stop me from doing what I always did. In a way, it was kind of amusing. I wasn't popular at all, and I didn't have any close friends, but through this cult thing, it was almost like they were all talking about me like I was cool and mysterious. For a while, I almost played along.

I'd arrange the leftover bones in creepy shapes, and I think I carved a pentagram into a rat once or twice. The buzz around this mysterious cult got so intense that our teachers banned us from discussing it in the school.

It was fun for a while, but when all was said and done it was a compulsion, one that didn't make me feel particularly good one way or the other. And I also thought to myself, why should they be a part of this most secret part of me? Yes, everyone thought that it was fun and games- if a little creepy, but if they found out it was *me*, that would all evaporate. So I took to carefully hiding the little bodies when I was done with them. No more playfully going along with the rumors.

Everyone tried to keep it going for a while, maybe they had completed their ritual, maybe it only happened once every ten years- I know that Alice tried to do some research and find out if there were any other incidents of bizarrely mutilated animals in the woods in years prior, but eventually it just kind of died out.

***

"Did they ever find out who or what it was?" Rachel asked, and licked her ice cream as we left the shop. I shook my head and finished my heavily abridged version of the cult story.
"Nope. Never." I said, maybe a little too clipped.

I had only gotten ice cream because she wanted some, and honestly, I was feeling rather sick. I feebly bit at it with my front teeth- my special talent- and was quiet. I had been gearing up to something, something that I was too cowardly to say out loud, and of course, she was wearing that blue jay pendant again. It was her favorite, after all.

Did she really need to know, though? I could just let it stay buried.

***

I don't quite remember how old I was. I think I might've been six. I was playing on the back porch, near the apple tree in my grandma and grandpa's backyard- it was the time of year where the tree made flowers instead of apples, which I remember finding amusing.

They had a cat, Dora, who always caught birds or rodents to eat. My grandpa claimed that once, she had killed and eaten a rabbit. I'm still not sure if he was just pulling my leg or not.

I looked up from my little toy cars when I heard a horrid squawking noise, and the sound of the grass around the tree being trampled and flattened. I remember gasping and looking up. I'd never seen Dora kill anything so up close. The blue jay kept almost getting away, Dora was having trouble getting a good grip on it. It was injured though, so no matter how it struggled, it couldn't fly right.

I rose to my feet, and yelled Dora's name. I shooed her away, and she sulked off while the blue jay struggled on the ground, flapping its broken wings desperately.

Getting down close to it, I could see so many details that I had never seen before, or even thought about before. I'd only seen birds close up in storybooks or postcards. I'd never thought about how strange the little black eyes looked, or just how delicately textured the feathers were. It kept up screeching, trying and refusing to give up its efforts to fly away. I picked it up- I was still young enough to not think about all the diseases wild animals carry around.

It was warm, soft, and squirming in my hands. I squeezed it a little, and I saw its beak open as its cries became deafening. Squeezing a little harder, and the rasping screeches were louder. I didn't like the noise. I squeezed it even harder until I started to hear cracks and pops, and the noise became strangled and weak. Its beak might've scared me a little bit, because when it twisted its head to peck at my hand, I squeezed as hard as I could, and it was dead.

I shook it around a bit, I played with it a bit. Poking with a stick, and the like.

I wasn't trying to be mean. I was just curious, I suppose.

After a while, I dug a hole with my hands and buried it. I don't know why I didn't just tell grandma and grandpa that Dora killed it, that seemed like something that would seem a suitable cover-up, for a six year old, anyway.

Years later, I offered to do yard work for my grandpa, but I was really just trying to find its thin bones, and take the skull for my box. I did find it, and it felt nice to have the first one.

***

We were sitting on some boulders, near the lazy summer Merced River. Rachel was tossing rocks into the river as the sun set. We'd made dinner at my apartment, and after eating we took a walk. This particular spot by the river was Rachel's favorite in town. It was quiet, and it wasn't a typical fishing spot for the old guys in town, and thankfully it didn't seem popular with teenagers sneaking off to smoke, either.

I shut my eyes. The sound of the river was soothing, but the little animal noises kept making my eyes jerk open to find the source. I saw squirrels running through the leaves, up tree trunks. I saw birds, flying through the trees and rustling the leaves. I'd been thinking too much about the old stuff I used to do. Usually, animals and the sort didn't remind me of it. But now, I felt that old feeling- sort of a queasy but excited feeling when I heard a little animal noise. I had the urge to follow them into the bushes and watch them until the moment was right. I almost rose to my feet at one point, but I kept gripping the rough bark of the log and stayed down. Maybe I seemed a little stiff, because Rachel noticed.

"What's up?" she tossed another rock into the river. "You're really quiet."

"You say I'm quiet all the time."

"Different quiet. Like something's bothering you. You've kinda seemed bothered all day, to be honest."

"I suppose so." I said, making a conscious effort to relax my shoulders.

For a few moments, Rachel was silent, her eyes gazing off into the sun dappled river. I always thought her eyes were the same color as those little brownish rocks at the bottom of the Merced River.

"If you're comfortable sharing what's bothering you, you should tell me. Especially if I did something." she said finally.

"You didn't do anything."

"Are you thinking about last night?"

"Kind of. But not in a bad way, I was just thinking that, we've kind of… things are kind of on another level. I was thinking about stuff about me, and stuff about you, and thinking that maybe we don't know a lot about each other." I said, saying more than I meant to.

Rachel made a "hmm" noise, and looked up at the leaves over our heads.

"There's always more to learn about a person." she said, tossing yet another stone. It made a deep *thwack* as it met the river.

"Here's something you don't know about me. When I was in middle school, this girl made fun of my old shoes, so I made up a rumor that she was into the school's main janitor. Like, *into* the janitor. It didn't really take off, but for about a week, people looked at her funny. So there, now you know something about me that isn't that great. Now you can share yours and not feel bad."

I looked Rachel in the eyes, though it was hard. I could barely resist glancing over at the little birds and squirrels, and thinking about all those times. Sometimes, I kind of miss my box, don't ask me why.

In the moment- that golden sunlight moment next to the river- I decided I would tell her. Right there and then. Rachel, would she leave? Would she hate me or think less of me? Would she think I was a freak? Why couldn't I envision any way this ended well?

But if I didn't tell her now, when would I ever tell her? Rachel loved birds and other animals so dearly, how could I be with her when at the same time hiding so much about who I was, and who I almost became?

I loved Rachel, and I couldn't just let those things stay buried. Buried, like bones in the forest.

When the Moon Disappeared

One day the moon disappeared.

No reason why, it just did.

I heard about mass panic, looting, and cults. My parents called me, worried about their safety. I told my mom, come up to my house, up in the coastal mountains, but she said no. Their little stubby-legged dog had run away, scared by noise. They wanted to wait for him, convinced he would come stumping back home like he always did when he got away. They loved that dog.

I understood that. My best friend was a cat, so it was probably hereditary. So often I would be focused so hard on my telescopes and research, forgetting to eat and sleep or brush my teeth until Neptune gently brushed against my leg.

I dote on that cat, and that cat dotes on me.

My fellow researchers were panicking. I got so many emails, both from my university and personal emails. One of my colleagues despaired and put a gun to his mouth. There wasn't a funeral, but I hung his obituary on the wall, and I lit a candle, too. It was the least I could do, even though we weren't close.

Neptune actually left it alone, that candle in its glass. It gave warm light to that corner of the living room, and flickered in my cat's eyes.

Not every natural consequence was terrible.

Yes, the tides were weak, and the days and nights were both not quite long enough, and it felt like you were constantly being gaslit by nature itself.

But it did snow on my cabin. In California in Mid-October.

One sunset I turned off the news as another story about a cult's human sacrifices came up, and I sat quietly with Neptune by the window. We admired the snow glistening in the waning sunlight.

Then she showed up, walking through the snow in a flimsy white dress with matching white slip-on shoes. She shivered but said it was fine, that it was colder where she was from.

I invited her in and gave her tea. She insisted that it wasn't car trouble when I asked.
Her hair and eyes were dark, incredibly dark, contrasting with her pale, pale face. Her face had these faint marks; they reminded me of old acne scars. The pattern was oddly familiar.

She spoke at length, she was so talkative. The woman spoke about the snow, how beautiful it was, and the birds, how small and musical they were. She became so excited when Neptune silently walked in on smoky gray feet. She picked him up and pet him with no hesitation.

I was surprised. Neptune seldom met other people, and upon the rare occasion I had guests, she would run away and hide under my bed until they had left. Sometimes I wanted to join her down there, even when I liked my guests.

I asked the woman where she was headed. She spoke energetically, listing so many places. I don't want to stay in the same place for too long, she said. I don't want to miss anything.

So, she's terminally ill, or a felon on the run, I thought.

Not many people have such a positive outlook, I said.

She replied, holding the mug of tea in her white hands.

How can I not, when everything is so lovely?

But everything isn't lovely, I said, and thought about the shotgun lying loaded under the bed. I hadn't had to use it, but my mom was scared of cultists in the area, and made me promise I'd keep it loaded.

The woman glanced off to the side, running a finger along the smooth ceramic surface of the mug.

But the good outweighs the bad, she said.

I had to confess, it was hard to look at it that way. I asked her if she had encountered any trouble in the cities, and what it was like where she was from.

She told me she hadn't really given much heed to smoke on city skylines, or freeways congested with cars fleeing the cities.

She said, I always thought that city lights were pretty, like clusters of stars. But now I have the chance to see one up close, I don't really want to.

Her voice was a little sad.

I asked if she was from a rural area, and she merely said that she was from far away.

I've heard, she said, that cities are often like this, with fighting and all that.

I sipped my tea and said something like, it's worse now, since the moon's gone and scared everyone here. You're being safe, right? I asked, and continued. There's cults up in the mountains and maybe even here, it's dangerous to travel alone.

She put her mug down with a clatter, surprising Neptune, who leapt off her lap.

Do you have music here? She asked abruptly.

I put on a record, some classical music on vinyl, Debussy, I think. Something on piano.

She stood by the window, lilting back and forth on her heels. It was dark by then. I joined her to look through the trees at the starry but moonless sky.

I'm an astronomer, I said. Do you want to see anything through my telescope? I said on a whim.

Show me your favorites, she said, her eyes sparkling like the Pleiades.

Show me the Andromeda Galaxy, the Eagle Nebula, and Saturn and its moons.

I wondered how she knew my favorites.

With Neptune slinking around our feet, I showed her upstairs.

I usually hiked up the mountain a little, sweating with all my gear in a duffle bag slung across my back and a heavy tripod in my hands. Lately though, I started to set up on a flat part of my roof.

I already had the telescope set up, I'd put it up there before I made dinner so I wouldn't have to in the dark. No light plus climbing around on a roof with a heavy telescope is a recipe for disaster.

Wow, look at how big the sky is, look at how many stars there are. She exclaimed, throwing her arms up above her head as she craned her neck. I had to grab her wrist, she was too close to the edge and wasn't paying attention to her feet.

Stay away from the edge, I said, brushing a thin layer of snow off the telescope with my other hand.

This is the best place to see the stars from, she said. This is the absolute best.

She liked breathing hot air out of her mouth and watching it cloud up in the air, and tracing patterns with her finger in the frost on my tripod.

Never seen snow before? I asked.

Never up close. She replied.

I looked at her face, obscured in shadow but near glowing from anticipation.

Hold on a second, I said, peering through the viewfinder and looking for Saturn. This would be a good one to start with, so distinctive and familiar.

I remembered the first time I had seen Saturn through a telescope. I'd so far only been able to find the moon in my telescope- space appearing so much more vast when magnified. I couldn't even find Mars or Venus. Talking either to myself or to the moon, I would grumble about how it was the only thing I could find, or how its light was obscuring other things I was looking for. I wasn't, and still am not, a person who can just talk to anyone about what I feel, but the moon was a silent listener, and I shared everything with her without even realizing.

The day I first found Saturn, I whooped and pumped my fist. It was around midnight, and I remember my mom sleepily opening the window to ask me what was going on.

It's Saturn, I found Saturn, I cried.

It was so much more than just another dot in the sky. I could see the space between the ring and the planet's body, and that tiny detail alone made me tremble; this celestial body didn't just exist in picture books and NASA photographs. It was real, it was up there sitting in the sky, and I could find it and look at it.

Even now, fifteen years later, I felt an echo of the same thrill as I honed in on Saturn.

There, take a look, I said.

She inhaled in wonderment as she winked one eye shut and stood on her tip-toes so she could look through the lens.

I've never seen it so clearly, you can see the rings!

I don't know how long we were up there, I had left my phone downstairs and never thought to get it, which was a contrast to the rest of the week, when my phone hadn't left my hand.

I started to shiver, and get a runny nose. My fingers were starting to feel a slight chill even through my gloves, but her? In her thin white dress and white slip on shoes, she politely turned me down when I offered to get her a jacket. I even ducked back into the house and grabbed an extra one, but after holding it awkwardly for a few minutes, she put it down on the ground next to the tripod feet, apparently comfortable in the 34° Fahrenheit weather.

Can we look at other things on Earth with this? She asked.

I don't know if this telescope would work so well for that. I replied.

Then let's get off the roof, and look for something very small! She said, stars in her eyes. Her eyes were like two galaxies. I knew that they had seen stars- and space and comets and the planets spinning like tops. Somehow I knew.

Something very small? I asked.

Like a ladybug, or pebble. I want to see it all. We've looked at things that are very big and far away, now I want to see something very small and up close- something I can't look at from home.

Okay, I said, rather baffled. I knew why she wanted to see all those things, but I was pushing it to the back of my mind because it seemed silly.

We went back down indoors. The warm air stung my face- a good feeling that I was used to after spending time out in the chilly night air. I had to turn the lights on as we went back down to the living room, as I'd turned them all off to avoid light pollution.

Neptune was sitting on the sofa, curled into a perfect, gray circle. She regarded us through orange, partially opened eyes, that odd little sleepy glare that I noticed cats do sometimes.

I opened the front door, ready to go out, but as I stepped out onto the frigid patio, I realized that she hadn't followed me. I stepped back through the door, and saw her standing, looking down into the candle I had in front of my colleague's obituary. She picked up the candle and held it in both hands while she read the newspaper clipping I'd hung on the wall. A grainy picture of my colleague smiled up from the clipping.

That's my friend, I worked with him. I said. He died back when all this started.

All this… she said, trailing off. Why did he do it?

I was a little bit at a loss. Wasn't it obvious why?

Well, you know. I said. The whole thing with the moon.

She put the candle down and gazed into the flame. I saw her shoulders shake a little bit. I didn't say anything, waiting to see if she would say anything. She always listened to me, I wanted to do the same.

That's so sad, I didn't know. She said after what felt like a long time. Is the whole world really falling to pieces just because the moon disappeared?

It looks that way. I said. I wasn't good at finding comforting words for people. I wish I was like Neptune, and I could make people feel better by simply being there. I walked up to be next to her, and thought about putting my hand on her shoulder, but I didn't.

She leaned her head on my shoulder. It was surprisingly heavy and her cheek was cold. I put my arm around her, thinking maybe I *could* be like Neptune, and just be there for someone who wanted me to. Just like she'd been for me.

I always planned on going back. She said. I got tired of being all alone. I wanted to see everything that you see. Don't you ever get tired of being up here on this mountain, away from everyone else? Far away?

I don't know, maybe sometimes. I muttered. But you know, you're not completely alone if you still talk to people. Even if they're far away, I can still talk to my parents, and I don't feel cut off from them. Maybe you just need someone to talk to, even if they're far away.

She made a small *hmm* noise as she kept leaning on my shoulder.

You should tell me everything you see in a day. She said. Everything you see, everyone you meet.

I will.

The woman took her head off my shoulder, and looked into my eyes.

You will?

Yes.

She nodded and walked out onto my front porch, and I followed. Her feet made a soft, muffled noise on the snow as she stepped off the porch. I thought about following her, but I stayed on the wooden steps. She turned around and waved goodbye. It didn't seem like a goodbye forever kind of wave. Just the kind of wave you give someone when you know you'll see them around in a day or two. I waved back. I wanted to say something else, but I didn't.

She'd never asked my name, and I had never asked hers. It didn't matter though, we already both knew. We'd known for a long time.

The Masquerade

A bubbly, pink rose was gracing Señora Maria Lucia's lips when she first heard whispers of him.

"When do you suppose the count will arrive?"

She turned to look down the table at the speaker. He was a young man with a thin mustache and a plain black party mask. He was speaking to another party-goer selecting a glass of wine.

"What count?" he asked, rather confused. Though she'd already picked up a glass, Maria didn't move away from the table, even when people were awkwardly reaching around her for rose, and the servant had filled in gaps on the table with freshly filled glasses.

"You know! The count! Juan Felipe Diego de Guzman!" said thin mustache.

"Well, what is he the count of?"

Thin mustache scoffed.

"Does it matter? He's amazing. Nobody knows where he came from or who his family is, but he's got this massive estate up in the Santas Piedras area. My cousin, she works as a maid there. She mentioned that the place has been buzzing with excitement ever since the invitation arrived!"

"What invitation?" Maria finally intruded on the conversation, shouting a little over the noise as she 'polished' the jewel on her necklace with her index finger.

"Hmm?" asked thin mustache. "I beg your pardon?"

"I'm Maria Lucia Rodrìguez." she said as if that were the answer to a question. It took a moment before the young man and the one he'd been speaking to showed recognition.

"Oh!" said thin mustache.

"Where are my manners! Hello Señora Rodrìguez! Thank you for the invitation. Me and my wife were thrilled." said the other man.

"I'm glad to hear it." she said, unable to recall this gentleman's name.

"It's a pleasure to meet you in person, Señora. My apologies. I didn't expect someone so young to be our fine hostess." said thin mustache.

"You're talking about some count? I've never heard of him, and I most certainly did not write an invitation for him."

"Ah…" said thin mustache. He nudged the other man. "Did you have any servants fill out the invitations?"

"I filled out invitations for guests I'm acquainted with personally. I had help with all the others, of course, I can't imagine writing all this. But that's beside the point, because I had to approve the list beforehand." said Maria, folding her arms, the half-full glass of rose coming dangerously close to spilling.

"Hmmm, well, Juan, Felipe, Diego, all common names, right?" said thin mustache. He adjusted his mask and took another glass of wine from the table, this time a pinot noir.

"I don't remember a 'de Guzman'. I think you're just making this count up." said Maria. Thin mustache shrugged.

"Well, my friend." he said to the other man. "I must take my leave and say hello to some other friends. Maybe I'll even catch a glimpse of that count!"

"He's not-" thin mustache walked off with his pinot noir as Maria spoke. "- he's not real! My god, who was that even?" Maria asked the man, who was squinting to read the placards with the wine names.

"I um, I don't know. I didn't catch his name."

"Hm. Probably one of the Rodrigos. They were always social climbers, pretending to have affluent friends and the like. They think that having almost the same surname as us they can pass off as higher than they are." Maria sauntered off. Where was her husband, Armando? Probably off trying to request some silly song from the chamber orchestra. The crowd parted- not dramatically of course- for Maria as she waded through, her full, pink skirt giving her plenty of space to avoid bumping elbows with people. She heard a woman murmur something about a 'count', and her friend asking 'well what does he look like'? Maria turned around and tried to find the source of the chatter, but the two women had already been carried away by the tides of the crowd.

"Ah!" said Maria, finding Armando exactly where she guessed she would. "My love, why are you avoiding me?" she jested, grabbing his arm and leaning on his shoulder- squishing her skirt as she leaned in close.

"I'm waiting for this piece to end, I want to request a waltz. This is so slow and dreary!" said Armando. Quite a lover of music himself, Armando was hopelessly uncoordinated. He collected sheet music- had a whole library stuffed full of it- and every time they threw a party, he would dig out some obscure waltz or another and wait, with the parts in his arms, until he could jump in and give them to the ensemble.

"It's supposed to sound like that. It represents… anguish or something. It sounds out of place at a party, but I requested it because I heard good things about it. It's a selection from that new opera, you know, and it's *so* popular. Thought the guests might like to hear something they recognize."

"Oh…" said Armando. "Now you say it, it *does* sound familiar. This scene was dreadfully sad."

"Maybe I should've requested something from Act II instead."

The final bars of the piece were too quiet and despairing to be heard by the partygoers, but the chamber orchestra played them anyway, right up to the long hold on the final note- indicated in the score as *a note held for as long as grief lasts.*

"I've decided that tonight, grief only lasts twenty seconds-" said the conductor, winking at the concertmaster as Armando took his cue and dropped the score for *Der Rosenwalzer* on his music stand.

"Oh, hello Señor Rodriguez, this wasn't on the list given to us, we'll be sight reading."

"It's easy! My mother always had this play at her parties, and look, barely any markings on the music. That must mean that it's not terribly difficult, yes?"

The conductor glanced at Maria. Internally, she sighed, but out loud she just promised a small bonus for their trouble.

"Alright then, trust the lady of the house to come up with a wise solution! Alright everyone, *Der Rosenwalzer* and then the waltz requested by the Count!" the conductor said, handing the stack of parts to the concertmaster to distribute.

"What?"

"Why don't you ever put this on the list?" Armando asked, hooking elbows with Maria as the orchestra re-tuned.

"Mmm, I just forget, and what was that about a 'Count'? Did you see any count?" Armando shrugged, and just remarked on the piece.

"Ah, they sound wonderful! They're doing this such justice!"

Truth be told, she wasn't particularly fond of this ratty old piece. It was flouncy and stiff, surly and fantastical, cheerful yet morbid, all at the same time. Some might find it delightful, but for her it was disconcerting.

It's no wonder that this composer hardly ever gets played. Maria thought to herself as the chamber orchestra began. They were uncertain at first and it was audible that they were figuring it out on the fly, but after the first few bars, even Maria had to admit that they didn't sound *terrible.*

I do wish that the piece could just make up its mind about what it's all about! She thought as Armando wordlessly tugged her arm and they went to the center of the ballroom floor. He stepped on her toes a few times, and Maria switched their arms around so that *she* was in the lead. Their guests were used to Maria taking the more masculine role when dancing with her clumsy husband. Though he always tried to start out in the lead.

"You know, my love," Maria said, trying to make conversation as they danced, rather than listen to that din. "People keep talking about this 'count'. Juan Felipe Diego de Guzman. From Santas Piedras."

"Oh, yes! I haven't met him in person until tonight, but he was on our guest list."

"I don't remember putting him down for an invitation! I would've remembered!"

"Well, look around, love, we do have a lot of people here. Besides, he wouldn't have gotten in without an invitation. We can ask the doormen if they had any trouble tonight, if you like. After this piece, of course!" Armando tried to spin Maria around.

"Don't try to get fancy!"

"I would like to stay and dance to the waltz that the count requested."

"Why is everyone talking about this count like he's the most interesting, amazing person? Last I checked it wasn't his party." Maria added the last part quietly, inaudible underneath all the music and party noise.

After *Der Rosenwalzer* came to its bizarrely soft ending cadence, there was a brief pause in the dancing as everyone waited for the next thing to start. Then, a gentle flute solo wafted through the air like the scent of sweet rose petals.

Maria saw Armando react to somebody behind her, and a half second later, a man with a white gloved hand took hers and asked,

"May I have this dance?"

Maria turned around and saw a tall man- maybe unusually tall- with a simple black mask, decorated only with a peacock feather. His clothes were dark and simple as well, but so impeccably tailored that one couldn't possibly mistake him for anyone of low status. Maria's eyes flitted down to the hand that had taken hers. There was a gold ring on his finger, with the initials *DG*. Could this be- the *count?*

"Count de Guzman, or am I mistaken?" Maria asked.

"It is a pleasure to finally meet you, count! I have heard much about you." said Armando, as the orchestra took the peaceful melody from the flute and turned it into something a little faster, more tense. "Please, the pleasure is all mine, Señor Rodríguez." The count had a rather deep, full voice, but he didn't use it to sound commanding or intimidating. "Please allow me to have this dance with your lovely wife." he lifted Maria's hand to his lips.

"He's a perfect gentleman." said Maria. "Go and fetch us three glasses of wine, Armando. After this piece, maybe the three of us can spend some time getting to know each other."

"Yes!" said Armando, diving into the sea of people and disappearing.

Maria looked up at the count- he was a head taller than her, at least- and tried to get a look at his eyes through the holes in his mask. He perhaps had green eyes, though it was hard to tell in the lighting.

He took the leading role as the music crescendoed and an incredibly fast pattern was scattered throughout the instruments before a swinging, lilting waltz took over and the entire ballroom was in motion.

It had been a long time since Maria had felt like she was flying.

"You're a good dancer." she shouted over the music. The count smiled. He looked young, much younger than he had expected. He might've been her age or even younger. The count spun Maria around, and the momentum sent her right into his chest.

"It just takes practice." he said.

"No offense, count, but I don't recall writing you an invitation."

The suggestion of a frown crossed the lower half of the count's face- the half she could see unobscured, of course.

"There *are* a great many people here." he said. He took one hand away from her waist, and reached into his pocket. He drew out an invitation, exactly like the ones Maria had sent out, complete with the family seal, broken of course.

"Oh, my apologies." said Maria, not without some degree of confusion. "I just thought that… well, I don't know what I thought. I just didn't recall your name from the list."

"No offense taken, my lady! I have enjoyed your hospitality immensely."

"Thank you. Now, if you don't mind me asking, how exactly do I know you? You're too young to be a friend of my father, but neither me or my husband are acquainted with you. How did you end up on our guest list?"

"I ask myself the same thing when some Madame This or Signore That shows up at one of *my* parties." said the count, laughing musically. "I think that somehow, we all just end up on each other's lists. Recommended by a friend of a friend of a friend. The rich all know each other, even if they haven't met before."

"You speak as if you aren't one of 'the rich'." said Maria, amused as he spun her around by one arm. Her dress twisted tightly around her legs before ballooning out again.

"Nouveau-Riche, I think the French call it." he said, not even breaking a sweat despite the unusually fast pace of the waltz. "My father came upon his money in such an odd fashion, I don't bother telling the story anymore."

"You should tell me. I'm your hostess, and I'm interested in getting to know you better."

"The details are quite boring! Odd doesn't always equal interesting."

"You know, I've never encountered an oddity that *wasn't* interesting."

"I'll tell you while we have those drinks that Señor Armando was sent to fetch! If you don't mind my saying, you have quite the commanding presence! I don't think my father's mentor in the paint shops of Florence was that intimidating, and *he* was nicknamed the commandant for fu- for goodness sake!"

Maria raised an eyebrow as they glided across the shining ballroom floor. However he spoke in private, Maria didn't care, but one didn't often come across a count who spoke in public like a sailor.

"Did your father have trouble getting used to mingling in more… more sophisticated circles?"

"Certainly. Just as Armando over there would have no idea how to act in some London butcher shop."

"How about you? Do you ever feel challenged? Like you don't exactly fit in?"

"All the time!" said the count, not even breaking a sweat as the two glided across the dance floor. Even Maria, after all her dance classes and parties, was out of breath.

"Well, you're a magnificent dancer." she panted.

"I've had a lot of practice!"

Maria didn't think she could go on any longer- then the rollicking waltz came to its close just in time, the end heralded by flourishing cadences.

The gap between pieces was filled with the roar of chatter.

"Well!" said Maria as the orchestra started a much more laid back piece of music, "I've no doubt that you could keep on for hours, but I think I would like to have a bit of fresh air. Would you like to join me outside in the rose garden?"

The count nodded, looking around over her shoulder.

"Where is Señor Armando, though?"

Maria waved her hand dismissively.

"He'll be along. My husband is very easily distracted, he probably bumped into a friend and they're chatting away, his errand long forgotten. The first place he'll look is the rose garden, it's our favorite place, so we can go. It'll be fine."

The aroma of countless roses wafted like a gentle flute solo through the air as they went outside to the small garden courtyard.

"This is my favorite place." said Maria, sitting down on the edge of the fountain. She lifted her foot to loosen the strap on her shoe, just to give her tired feet a break. Her full skirt took up a foot on either side of her, but the count probably would've kept a respectful distance anyway. He even averted his eyes from her be-stockinged ankle.

"It's beautiful." the count replied, looking around, mouth slightly agape.

From the rose garden, they could see the side profile of the immense mansion, so many of the rooms lit up, glowing gold in the indigo night. It was so clean cut, so beautifully built and maintained, and while chatter from the ballroom drifted out, it felt more intimate a place than a library at midnight.

"I maintain most of the rose bushes myself. It's more than just a way to fritter away time, I really love it out here. And doing all the work makes me feel like it belongs exclusively to me. Do you know the feeling?"

"Hmm?" The count had been staring up at the sky as stars appeared out of the darkness, little by little.

"Ah! You weren't listening! I said, I maintain the rose garden myself, so it really feels like I own this little place."

"Oh… I do understand that feeling." he said, putting his hands in his pockets and looking a little over his shoulder at the fountain.

"I hear and sometimes I read in the papers that I'm considered rather vapid and spoiled. People don't appreciate all the work that goes into running a household like mine. My husband, he doesn't have a good head for numbers or business. I manage pretty much everything, while still being the pretty wife and gracious host. On top of all that, I keep this garden looking as beautiful as it does. But no, people don't think of it like that. They think, she's rich, she has everything, ergo, she is spoiled and horrible." she twisted one of the fine rings on her fingers.

"Hmmm…"

"Hmmm, what?" Maria said, leaning over and gently grabbing the count's chin and pointing his face back at her.

"I agree that you are much more nuanced than people think." he said, sounding so much more careful than he had before.

Maria laughed, a little taken aback.

"Well, thank you. I'm a 'little' more nuanced than people think. I can accept that."

"Oh no, don't take anything the wrong way, I'm just a little lost in thought." the count said hastily. "No, I agree. People who have nothing better to do than gossip, they're wrong."

"Do you um, have anything like this? A place that you've made your own? Something that servants and the like aren't allowed to touch?"

The count cocked his head to the side thoughtfully, and adjusted his mask as it slid down his nose. Maria reached back and untied the ribbon holding her own mask to her face, and felt cool air against the newly exposed skin.

"I suppose… when I travel. When I leave the estate, I like to go by myself. Tonight, I came in a small coach, just me and my driver. We're more friends than anything else. I like to take turns driving *him*. There's nothing like the wind in your face, especially at night time. It makes me wonder if my father felt more or less free after he became a wealthy man."

"I spent so much time imagining when I was small. Reading my books about princesses, thieves, and pirates, and thinking to myself, I would so much rather be a pirate than a fine young lady." Maria mused, fiddling with the ribbons of her mask, which sat on her lap. The count smiled a little, and untied his own mask. His face was a little different than she had imagined- his nose looked like it had been broken once- but it only made him more handsome in Maria's eyes.

"Tell me, count. I would like to know your favorite places to travel to." the temptation to snake her fingers around his was starting to become a little nuisance.

"Oh, well… There's too many. But I think my favorite has to be the coast. Have you ever ridden horseback on the beach? There was this one day… It was clear, just a smudge of cloud on the horizon, and the wind was something ferocious that day, let me tell you. That and the flecks of sea water stung my eyes so bad I could hardly keep them open, but for some reason it was the finest moment. Just the finest."

"Sounds lovely. This place is wonderful, but I would love to visit the seaside more often. I can't remember the last time Armando took me somewhere besides the city." Maria laughed, not without a hint of bitterness. "And when we *do* go to the city, it's not for fun. At least, not really what I think of as fun. Business dinners with this or that important person. If we're lucky, there's time to see the opera or the symphony."

"Hmmm."

Once again, the count's gaze drifted off into the dark sky. Rather than take hold of his chin and direct his gaze back to her, Maria said nothing and kept her eyes locked on him. What could be bothering him?

"You're so quiet all of a sudden."

The count looked down, fidgeting with his hands.

"I suppose I should go soon. I didn't expect to have such an enchanting time." he looked up and spoke without mumbling as a weak smile crossed his lips. "But unfortunately I have business to attend to early tomorrow, and I must go back."

"So soon...?" Maria felt her face fall, though she tried to disguise it.

"I planned on just stopping by for a little while. I've already stayed longer than I originally thought I would."

"But, Armando will be back soon with the wine-"

The count rose, and tied his mask back onto his face. He smiled and reached his hand down to Maria. She took his hand and stood, straightening out her gown with her other hand. Her mask fell to the ground- she had forgotten it was sitting on her lap.

"Oh," she reached down and picked it up. The count brushed against her, making an attempt to be the gentleman and get it before her.

"Allow me." The count took the mask, and stepping behind her he tied the delicate pink ribbons.

"Thank you. Are you sure you have to go so soon? So suddenly?" Maria asked, taking the count by the arm as he tried to walk back into the ballroom.

The count turned to her dolefully, but not without a vague and wistful smile.

"I'm afraid so. I have quite a ways to go, and I'm afraid that if I stay longer, I won't be able to leave."

"Then don't leave. You don't have to do anything that people expect you to. You can just be who you want to be."

The count was silent, gazing out into space past Maria's shoulder. She was just about to speak again, but he nodded and took her hand in both of his. He squeezed them affectionately as if they were childhood friends.

"Thank you, Maria. I hope to see you again, maybe the next time you have another one of your amazing parties."

Maria nodded vigorously, her earrings bouncing.

"And next time, there won't be any confusion about your invitation."

He didn't reply, but he kissed her hand and turned around.

The count put his hands in his pockets, and walked back into the party, looking up and catching a last glimpse of the night sky from the rose garden. Maria didn't know why she didn't follow him. She watched, stock still as he disappeared into the crowd.

Chase after him! Make that grand, romantic gesture you've always dreamed of.

But Armando emerged from the party, walking slowly, with three glasses of dark wine balanced in his two hands.

"Hello, my love. I was sidetracked by some guests, and when I finally got away, I dropped the glasses, so I had to go back and get more!"

Maria laughed and shook her head, wrapping one arm around her midsection, and putting the other to her neck to fiddle with her pendant.
It wasn't there-!

"Huh?" she said, looking around her feet, lifting her skirt above her ankles and shaking it, to see if it was caught somewhere.

"What's wrong?" Armando passed her a glass of wine. "And where did the count go?"

"My necklace fell off. Armando, help me find it!"

"Love, it's on the fountain edge."

Maria whirled around, and a wave of relief crashed over and extinguished the brief spell of panic.

"Ah. So it is."

The large jewel was positioned in the middle of a neat spiral made by the chain.

"How did it get like that?" Armando asked.

Maria wordlessly sat down and put her glass aside. She started to fasten the necklace, but her gloves were making it difficult, and she fumbled.

"I'll get it." said Armando, taking it and fastening it. He patted the back of her neck awkwardly, and kissed it. Despite her confusion over the necklace, a giggle escaped her lips. Those tiny, awkward gestures were so silly, but nothing made her want to dive onto him in a fit of passion like those clumsily romantic gestures.

"Where did the count go? I was looking forward to getting to know him. Everyone seemed so excited that he was here!"

"He had to go." said Maria, fingering the necklace in what was almost a trance. By far the most expensive piece of jewelry she owned. Left sitting in a perfect spiral on the fountain's edge.

***

Thin mustache was hunched at the boot of the coach, parked just outside the gates under the cover of the dark trees. Diego de Guzman could just barely make it out in the dim moonlight. When thin mustache saw him coming, he immediately started waving.

"Hey!" he half-called, half-whispered. "Hey, am I glad to see you! The goods that I grabbed are in the coach, take a look."

Diego silently opened the door and pulled himself up and in. There was a sack on the opposite seat, lying on its side with shining silverware spilling out. Thin mustache *always* threw the goods into the carriage without any care.

"Hey." Diego heard thin mustache hop down from the boot. Thin mustache put one foot on the step and put both hands on either side of the entrance. "What did you get? Why are you so quiet? Did something go wrong on your end?"

Diego shook his head and untied his mask. His brother raised his eyebrows as he swayed back and forth slightly- a little drunk from the party.

"Nothing went wrong. I just wasn't in the mood."

"Not in the mood? Tch! Whatever, Diego. You'd better be in the mood next time, because I don't think we're gonna get filthy rich just by selling fancy silverware. Though, to my credit, it's pretty nice silverware." He threw the door shut, and the coach jolted as he hopped back up onto the boot.

Diego sat back and looked out the window as the reins snapped and the coach shuddered into motion. The woods slid past, deep and dark.

It was too dark to take out his journal and check the plans for next week, but Diego could remember.

The Rodriguez Family Estate, family matriarch's birthday party. The target? The giant amethyst ring that adorned Señora Filomena Lucia de la Cruz's finger. It wouldn't be an easy steal, but Diego could do it.

Or rather, the *count* could do it.

Angels

Tristan had never been down in the deepest level of the dungeons before- never in all his time as a castle guard. That twisting maze, after all, was reserved for the prisoners who warranted some sort of *special* treatment. Everyone knew what went on, of course, but nobody really saw the need to discuss such unpleasantness, and when they did, they called it simply being visited by the information man.

To actually see this place with his own eyes was different from whispering about it up on the battlements. He stole glances at the cells as he passed by, escorted by a guard, and felt cold as he regarded the devices and imagined what each one could do.

"You'd better be sure you don't spill anything secret to the lads upstairs."

"Huh?" Tristan said, looking ahead at the back of his escort.

"I know they're gonna ask about it. The lads, you know? I know you lot are pretty talkative up on the sunny side of things. Make up any creepy, operatic details you want, as long as it isn't, well, literally anything it says."

"Okay. I wasn't going to anyway. Thank you, though."

"Can't blame everyone for being curious. Hell, this is historic, if you ask me. Can't imagine what it's like for you, I mean, you're the one who shot it down! That's pretty astounding."

Tristan put his hands in his pockets and looked down at the slightly damp stone floor as he went. For a moment he thought that he put the wrong shoes on that morning, but then he remembered.

I'd rather not wear my uniform when I go to see it.

"What're you going to say to it?"

"I don't- I don't really know."

"Well…" The guard paused by an iron door that looked no different from all the others. "This is it." he said in a quieter voice than before. He took a large ring with many keys off his belt and started flipping through them.

"Right." Tristan said, looking awkwardly off to the side.

"So you're sure you want to do this?" the guard asked, the key in the lock. Tristan wanted to roll his eyes.

For the last time, yes!!

The guard grimaced, a little nervous after all under all that nonchalance.

It can't hurt us. Not injured like it is.

Tristan nodded, and the guard twisted the key and pulled the iron bolts- all three of them, which were spaced evenly from the top to bottom of the door.

"I'll be right out here, just pull the rope by the door to ring the bell when you're done, or if there's any trouble. Oh, and it's pitch dark in there, go ahead and take this." the guard handed him a lit lantern with a tall, fresh candle in it. "For obvious reasons, we didn't want it in a cell with any daylight."

"Okay." said Tristan, taking the lantern and stepping into the darkness.

The guard didn't say anything else as he shut the door behind Tristan.

For a few moments, the light from the lantern was all he could see as his eyes adjusted. Then, the room gradually took shape around him, cast in shades of black and dim gold from the flame. The first thing he made out was a chain hanging from the ceiling, ending in a hook just above eye level in the middle of the cell. Tristan hung the lantern on the chain.

The cell was small and the floor was damp, water pooled in the cracks between the stones. There were various torture instruments about, hanging neatly on the wall while covered in blood. Tristan didn't really take in much else about the room, because then he saw the prisoner, crumpled at the wall directly across from the door.

The angel's arms were chained above its head- those chains also bolted into the ceiling. Its head was bowed, and it seemed unconscious, slumped in a kneeling position as low as the chains on its wrists would allow.

Tristan stepped a little closer. His eyes were drawn to the single downy wing just visible behind its strained, raised arms.

"We've got a surprise for you, Tris! Take a look!"

They handed me something wrapped in a bloody cloth. I already knew what it was as they handed it to me, but I unwrapped it anyway.

"A little souvenir, right?"

I didn't answer him. I tried to fake a smile, but looking at that severed wing- it filled me with an odd feeling that I couldn't quite put my finger on. Wasn't it a good thing that I did? I guess I'm here in the cell now trying to still figure that out.

Unsure of what to do, Tristan simply stood there, staring at the angel for a while. It had only been there for a day-

(Could it really have just been a day?)

-but the torturer had already been down there. It appeared dreadfully injured, covered in fresh, deep gashes, countless bloody *Xs* carved into its pallid skin. Tristan noticed the metal band around its neck, and recognized it as part of an interrogation method preferred by their main torturer.

A metal collar, welded shut and nigh impossible to remove. The ring on the back can be attached to any manner of devices, and doesn't just serve a practical purpose, it also goes a long way toward subjugating the criminal and lowering their mental fortitude.

The angel had a deep, angry looking burn on the back of its neck from the process of welding the collar around its neck, and it made Tristan wince and put his hand to the back of his *own* neck.

It felt like Tristan had been standing there for a little too long. He was beginning to think he should just leave, and was actually rather relieved that the angel hadn't awakened since he entered.

Tristan raised his hand to take the lantern down, but it was a little stuck. As Tristan fought with the metal hook, the slight noise and flickering of the candle seemed to awaken the angel. Tristan saw it stir and jumped back, the lantern swinging slightly on its chain.

"Hello." He said, realizing the absurdity of greeting it so casually.

The angel groaned and shifted, sitting with its back against the wall. It didn't look up, rather, it seemed too weak to lift its head.

Tristan cleared his throat a little, not really to get its attention, but because he felt like his throat was clogged with phlegm all of a sudden.

"Uh, hello. My name's Tristan. What's… what's yours?"

Do angels even have names?

The angel was breathing heavier than it had been when unconscious, and was recoiling, as if pressing its head against the cold stone wall would offer some respite from the pain it was in. Tristan felt a pang of sadness for it, even if it *was* an angel, after all- seeing something in pain up close was awful, especially knowing that it was because of him.

"Tristan, it's okay, it's mercy."

When I was twelve, my grandfather took me outside the city. He was teaching me how to tell the difference between poisonous and edible plants and mushrooms. We found a wild dog that had apparently lost a fight with a bigger animal. It was dying, insides spilling out onto the dirt. For some reason, I kept thinking about how uncomfortable it must be to have twigs and dry leaves stuck to your guts.

Grandfather broke its neck without a second thought. I was too sensitive, I was crying, just like I'm almost crying now. He put his hands on my shoulders and promised me it was mercy.

I wish they hadn't made me check in my knife before descending into the dungeon.

But wait, we need it to talk, don't we? That's why they are keeping it alive. If I killed it, they would probably kill me too. I've had coworkers executed for less than that.

Tristan approached the angel and knelt on one knee, the dampness seeping through the fabric of his pants. He reached out one hand and brushed its hair out of its eyes. Its eyes were bloodshot, and one of them nearly swollen closed, but Tristan could still make out the clear, deep violet of its irises.

"I'm the… I'm the one who shot you out of the sky. That morning was the first time I'd ever held one. They call it a firearm. It's clunky and hard to handle, but they told us it was our best chance against the angels for whenever they came back. So… when a scout saw you all coming down from the Boreal Mountains, they brought them out. I guess the practice paid off, right?"

The angel was awake. Tristan could tell from how it was breathing, and the way its eyes were carefully avoiding him, despite seemingly staring out into space.

"When I saw my shot hit you, it was like time stopped. I don't know if you've ever felt that. This is probably going to sound like I'm horrible. But when I saw the blood, when I saw you falling with one of your wings blown off, I started to… I felt relieved. I thought to myself, we can be safe now. Your friends retreated, and all my buddies were celebrating, drinking, picking out the prettiest whore at the pub to take to a room. I didn't feel too good, though. Even with the relief, I felt bad somehow. Even though you all… well, you're like monsters."

Grandfather used to tell me about it. When he was six, the angels came to Donabela, just like they did the other day, seventy-five years later. He told me about how he hid under a bench when the angels' divine light flooded the street and turned everyone to stone. He said it was beautiful in a way, they would fold their wings in front of themselves, charging a ball of light. Then they thrust their wings and arms back, releasing the light. His mother had shoved him under the bench, but before she could hide with him, the divine light turned her to stone. When everything was quiet, when almost everyone was dead, grandfather crawled out from under the bench and shook his mother. She crumbled into dust, as did the others when the next strong wind came.

"You only leave a few children. According to the legends, and my grandfather. He was little when you last came. Were you alive back then?"

"No."

Tristan jumped, almost losing his balance and tipping over. The angel was still avoiding his gaze, but spoke again.

"I couldn't fly yet during the last crusade." the angel spoke in a hoarse whisper, its voice cutting out sometimes, like a pianoforte with missing keys.

"You were a child?"

The angel nodded slightly.

"Huh." Tristan found himself bemused. "I didn't know that angels started as children. We don't know anything about you guys. But I suppose you guys know a lot about *us*. Enough to make you think it's okay to come and destroy us every century or so?"

The angel shut its eyes.

"I know that your civilization thinks it's okay to sacrifice infants to your gods. I know that your disabled are sold to the rich to be used as toys. I know that… that your kings only think about conquest and slaughter. You're a… you're a blight on this planet. You have to be punished until you realize that you've been in the wrong." its voice rose in anger, transcending the pain and fatigue.

Tristan felt cold. It was a little while before he knew what to say.

"That's not everyone. The priests, they only make sacrifices so that we have deliverance from the angels. It's hardly ever *infants*, but if it is, it's only ones that… that wouldn't have had a life anyway… It's considered merciful. It's considered an honor." To be honest, he hadn't really given it that much thought. "It's not a common occurrence. Only during holy seasons."

"I don't know what it is about your kind. But no matter how many times my ancestors struck you down and gave you another chance, you just rose again and got *worse*. Each and every time, you got worse. Never learning from the warnings left behind."

"So the solution is to destroy us? How does that make you any better? People died yesterday. Maybe I regret not hitting you sooner. I should've practiced more."

The angel slumped back down.

"Why am I still alive?" it asked. "Are you here to kill me?"

Tristan shook his head. Speaking with it was making him feel more secure in his actions. Shooting it out of the sky was the right and just thing to do. It was a pity that the guards wouldn't let him slit its throat right now.

"You know, I kind of wish I was. After learning what a horrible, disgusting thing you are. Who put you in charge, anyway? Who gave you the right to decide we all have to die?"

The angel lifted its head with difficulty, golden hair falling over its eyes. It looked Tristan in the eye, and its gaze made him uncomfortable. Tristan felt like he had to control what he was thinking, *lest he be judged,* or something like that.

"Maybe… maybe purifying a city from a distance is the same thing as shooting something down from a distance. When I was a child, I didn't dream of this. It was more like… a necessary duty that all of us growing up knew about, and knew that someday we would be called to purify. Believe me when I say this isn't what I dream of."

Tristan exhaled, a half-laugh.

"What exactly would an angel dream of growing up to be?"

"Nothing you'd consider interesting."

"Try me."

The angel slumped back down.

"I don't feel like talking about it." it said. The stump of a wing, just barely visible behind its shoulder, was twitching slightly.

"Oh… well, for what it's worth, this isn't exactly what I wanted when I was a little kid, either. I wanted to be a knight, not a glorified bouncer."

The angel didn't respond. Tears were making tracks through the grime on its face. Tristan's expression fell, and he looked away.

"There's something that was bothering me. You hesitated. I was able to shoot you down and not any of your friends because you were just hovering there. Staring at something on the ground. Basically a sitting duck in the middle of the sky. I'm not as good a shot as my friends say." Tristan stifled a laugh. "But that's why I'm here- I shot down the one angel in the sky who *wasn't* killing anyone. Even though you probably *would've* eventually, I still feel odd about it. I was hoping that maybe… maybe…"

"Like I said." The angel murmured. "This isn't what I dreamed of. I'm only here because I hate what you do. When the time came however… I found it more difficult than I had been led to believe."

"Hmm." Tristan rose to his feet. He felt a little lightheaded, and figured it was time to leave.

He'd satisfied his morbid curiosity, though it hadn't done anything to answer all the questions in his mind.

"If it makes you hate us a little less, that's how everyone feels about the sacrifices and martyrs. Nobody really wants to do it."

"Then why do you?"

Tristan had his hand raised, ready to ring the bell. He didn't answer, and tugged the rope.
A few clicks of the locks later, the door opened and even the dim lighting in the dungeon hall seemed bright to Tristan. The guard peered over Tristan's shoulder out of curiosity, but didn't hesitate to shut the door, at least.

He walked Tristan up, only breaking the silence a few minutes later to ask how it went. The answer was unsatisfactory and non-committal.

***

"What's the matter, Tristan?" asked Pippa. The night was cold and rainy, with wind howling and battering the windows. They were huddled under the covers, faces just visible in the light filtered through the fabric.

"Nothing's wrong." Tristan said, stroking her face. He realized that he had forgotten to put his ring back on after pocketing it before the dungeon. For some reason, he hadn't wanted the angel to know that he just got married.

"What happened at the meeting?" she asked hesitantly. Pippa knew that she wasn't *really* supposed to ask questions like that, but there had been something off about Tristan ever since the angels were chased away, and especially since he was summoned to the castle that day. Everyone else was celebrating. Angels had *never* been chased away before, it was like a miracle! And her Tristan was the cause of that miracle. Nobody was more proud than Pippa. She doubted that even his mother was as starstruck as she at this very moment.

"It was boring. Same old stuff I've been repeating since yesterday. And it's not going to stop there, probably. I'll be going down there tomorrow, actually."

Pippa snuggled even closer, tangling her legs with his.

"Why can't they just let you relax a little?"

"Well, the angels'll probably come back soon. Everyone's worried, y'know?"

"The way I see it, everyone's ecstatic."

"At the castle, I mean. They know that we need to be ready, and that they can't waste any time." he planted a kiss on her hair.

"Hmm." said Pippa. "I've been meaning to ask…"

"What?"

"Is it still alive? The angel? I thought I heard people talking on the street, saying it was alive and being held in the castle. For questioning, I think?"

Tristan didn't answer right away.

I don't want to talk about this, why can't I just be slightly better at acting? It's like she can already tell what's bothering me.

"Yeah, it's alive."

"Wow." she said quietly. "... what do you suppose they're doing to it? Have you seen it?"

"I might see it tomorrow. After the meeting…" Tristan said distantly, his voice feeling like something far away and out of his control.

"Wow… give it a kick from me, will you? Why is it still alive?" she said with venom lining her soft, bell-like voice.

Tristan shifted a little. His shoulder was cramping. He thought of the angel's severed wing.

How painful is it, I wonder.

"They think we can learn something from it. You know, maybe we can prevent another attack."

"You really think it'll talk?"

"It might."

"If they do half the things to it that they do to thieves, then it had better talk." Pippa snuggled close and buried her face in his neck. Tristan reciprocated and tightened his arms around her.

"I'll do what it takes to keep you safe, don't worry about the angel."

***

"**D**id you hear, Tristan? About the angels flying around the mountains?" asked the same guard from before. Tristan shook his head, but he wasn't surprised. Of course they were going to come back-but not without caution.

We showed that we can shoot them down, their wings are obsolete. They're no safer than us, and they know it. I knew I was right, we can't sit around and do nothing, just assuming they won't come back. They're probably frantically planning something right about now. But I guess I'm not high up enough to get invited to that *meeting. I'm sure I'll get told what to do once they know what. If they know what.*

"Yep. I heard." Tristan finally said, after taking just a bit too long to answer. He was staring at his shoes again as they trod on the damp, dungeon floor.

"Why is it that you're going to see the angel again? If you don't mind me asking."

"Curious, y'know. I just feel like talking to it again. I heard that it didn't talk."

"Pfft! Yeah. The information guy was down here all night, working harder than I've ever seen, but it didn't give him anything. I don't really think it'll tell you anything, just so you know. Last night was the worst I've heard in a while. I know *I'd* have talked. So you know... just don't get your hopes up.

The guard unlocked the door much more casually than the day before.

"Same as before, yeah? I'll be right here." Tristan noticed a tattered novel sitting on the guard's wooden stool.

"You'll be reading?"

The guard smirked and motioned for him to go inside the pitch dark cell.

It took a moment for Tristan's eyes to adjust to the light- at first he felt like his lantern was just making it *harder* to see, as the light was almost blinding. Not without a little bit of difficulty, he found the chain again and hung the lantern.

As his eyes adjusted, Tristan felt his shoulders stiffen, and his stomach jumped. He was just a guard. He didn't usually see the aftermath of the information man's sessions. The angel's swollen eyes made it hard to tell if it was awake or not, but it lifted its shaved head at the sound of Tristan hanging the lamp, random curly locks that were missed still dangling pathetically. It had a massive burn wound on the side of its head, and Tristan thought that its ear might've been gone.

"Hello." he finally said, cringing inside at the nonchalance of his own voice.

The angel murmured something that Tristan didn't understand. It was slumped against the wall, arms still chained above its head. Tristan could see huge purple and red bruises on its chest and stomach. Its ribs were probably broken. There were feathers on the floor, Tristan realized, and he noticed that fistfuls of down were missing from its remaining wing.

"You didn't say anything to the information man." Tristan said in a stilted voice.

"Izzat what he's called?" the angel slurred. "What does he want?"

Tristan wasn't sure how to respond. Come to think of it, it *did* seem silly to treat an angel like a human soldier, to ask it what its leaders were planning, to demand squadron formations and attack plans…

"He wanted to know what the others are planning… like when they're coming back?" the angel said with difficulty. "But I don't know any of that. Anything I know is useless… I can't even hear what they're thinking."

"You can usually hear that?"
The angel nodded slightly.

"If I concentrate very carefully, maybe they can hear me, but I don't think they want me to hear them. Maybe they think I would tell the- information man, was it?" The angel coughed, the air passing through his lungs making a hollow, rattling noise.

"*Have* you tried to tell them anything?" Tristan asked when the angel's coughing fit retreated.

"What exactly would I tell them?" It seemed a little offended. "That this cell is very dark and not really that nice? Oh, and that they keep-" cough- "Hitting me and asking questions that don't make sense?" More coughing.

Tristan regretted asking that.

Why am I back here? What do I really want to speak to this thing about?

"I don't know how long ago it was." It said hoarsely. "But at some point, the last time the information man was here, I prayed to them. To come and rescue me. It's silly. Like I'm a child, or something. Even if they heard me, they won't come for me. I feel like they'd rather destroy the city and me inside it. I'm not really worth it, huh. Just one wing. I'm sure that's what they all have nightmares about."

It just told me more than it's ever told the information man, hasn't it?

Tristan sat down on the damp stone floor.

"Last night, I told my wife that I would protect her. I don't like to say stuff I know I can't follow up on. I came down here because... I wanted to convince you to tell them what you know. After hearing you talk about how you can communicate with the other angels, though…"

The angel was silent. Though it was avoiding eye contact, Tristan persisted in gazing directly at its eyes.

"Tell them that there's good people here. Tell them that…"

No, that won't work… just look at him. Are they supposed to believe that it was just his fall that did all that to him?

"No… Tell them we'll let you go if they promise not to come back. Just give us a chance to get better. Maybe we don't have to be cut down, or maybe being cut down over and over again is what's making this happen. Making us build a culture the way we do… I don't know. But this hasn't been working. It's time for *something* to give, and I won't have it wait until after Pippa is dead!"

The angel was silent.

"I've spoken to you twice, and I feel like we could be friends if things were different. But before this, I never thought of you or yours like that. I wonder if the others could. Before I came here… I hated you all for being so sinful."

"But even after all this, you don't hate us as much?" Tristan asked, quietly baffled.

The angel slightly lifted one shoulder and made a non-committal face.

"I feel sorry that you're all so scared that your culture has something like the information man. I keep thinking that I hate *him*, but… well, it's easy to say that I don't hate him when he's not here, right?

I'm sure that next time he comes, I'll be eating my own words-" the angel broke out into hollow, raspy laughter that devolved into a coughing fit.

"... Okay. Well, if praying to them won't convince them not to come back, then I guess there isn't any good we can do, is there."

"Hmm?" The angel looked up, eyes watering as he recovered from his coughing fit.

"I've gotta go." Tristan said, and hastily rang the bell. There was nowhere he wanted to be *less* than this cell. What did he think he was going to accomplish by coming back to that awful place?

***

I was just roused from sleep by Pippa. As I blink away sleep, she tells me that one of my coworkers is here, and that I need to come with him. That's odd, according to the clock hands it is 3 in the morning, but there is light flooding in though the window, regardless of the time. It fades away as I sit up, and the room feels even darker than it must've been before, given the absence of the blinding light.

The angels have left something- right at the gate to our city. My coworker, well, one of my superiors, Sir Lwaithe, he says that initial reports say that it's a monolith. A tall slab of marble that reads

FREE THE ANGEL. WE RETURN IN TWELVE HOURS.

All are called to battle stations. Doubling down. The men stationed tonight fired at the angels as they arrived just outside the wall, seemingly out of nowhere. They didn't take any of them down, in fact, the angels succeeded in murdering three guards as they decimated a section of the wall.

*There is something else, I hear, on the other side of the
monolith. Sir Lwaithe begs me not to tell anyone else.*

THERE IS NO SALVATION FOR THOSE WHO HARM AN ANGEL

*****

Tristan's feet slipped as he sprinted down the
dungeon stairs, but he didn't fall. He didn't have the
guard to guide him- everyone was at their emergency
posts- but he knew the way. He hadn't hesitated to
bolt away from his post, for better or worse.
Well, first, he had gone to the castle shrine to pray,
but as he knelt, he heard the overseers discussing
what sort of sacrifices would satisfy the gods, and he
felt a sudden wave of discomfort. In his heart, Tristan
knew that no deaths would stop doomsday from
coming. They never really had done anything, had
they? No matter who died on an altar, history showed
that the angels came back as if there was no point.
What, then? If not sacrifices, then what?

The answer came to him as he nearly fell
asleep on his knees. The overseers hadn't noticed
Tristan was there until he was sprinting out of the
shrine.

His breath, his footsteps, the air rushing past
his ears- it felt like those sensations would never end,
but, led by memory and intuition, Tristan found
himself at the angel's door.

He reached for the door handle, but realized
that he didn't have any keys.

That would prove a significant barrier, now, wouldn't it.

"Hey, that you?" Tristan jumped.

It was his old friend the guard.

"Why are you here?" The guard asked nervously. "Should you be-"

"I need your help. Can you give me your keys, then run away from here as fast as you can?"

"But-" the guard shook his head. "You're going to free it, aren't you? I don't know much, but I do know that the king has no intention of caving to the angels. They're just gonna kill us anyway. You should know, you're one of the guards, isn't everyone getting a firearm for the assault-"

"None of your business, just run away. Please?"

"Some people tried to flee the city this morning. The angels turned them to stone and then they crumbled. I can't run away from whatever stupidity you're planning!"

"Just go home!" Tristan's hand flew to the sword on his belt. He was surprised at how readily he resorted to threatening the guard, but he knew he wouldn't really do anything. As long as the guard believed it, though… The guard's eyes stayed fixed on the glimmer of the blade in the dim lighting.

He sighed and lowered his chin.

"Okay, Tristan. I guess even if you've gone off the deep end, it doesn't matter." he unclipped his keys from his belt and dropped them into Tristan's outstretched hand. The keys felt jarringly cold.

"Thanks. I mean it. Go away, okay? If you get the chance, can you make sure Pippa stays put? I- I told her to stay with my mom, but I'm sort of worried she'll run out or something. She doesn't like being told what to do, y'know?" He scribbled his mother's address down on a scrap of paper from his pocket and handed it to the guard.

"... okay. I'll make sure." he turned, but hesitated. "Why're you doing this, do you really think it'll save us?"

Fumbling with the keys a little, Tristan stuck it in the lock and twisted. He paused, eyes closed and his forehead bumping against the door.

"I don't know."

The guard waited, as if wanting to hear something else, but Tristan didn't really have anything else. The guard walked at first, but broke out into a run, disappearing into the darkness- the last Tristan saw of him was his lantern's faint light.

He pulled the- surprisingly- heavy door open, and slipped inside, but not without propping the door open with the guard's wooden stool.

The scant light from the torches in the hallway was of no more help to Tristan, once the door closed. Every previous visit, he had had the lantern from the guard. As he fumbled around for some matches in his pocket, Tristan spoke. He questioned why he was so short of breath.

"Hey, are you still alive in here?" he asked, upon hearing nothing- either speech or motion- for a few seconds. He figured that if *he* were the one in captivity, he would jump and be alert every time some unknown person intruded on his cell. After all, it means either food, freedom, or more pain. All much more interesting and in a way reliving than the monotony of being kept in the dark.

Tristan asked again, trying and failing to strike up a match. They were so frail- stupid free matches from some pub.

"Hello? Angel, are you here still?"

Maybe they moved it. What do I do if they moved it?!

The sudden flare of the match roaring to life didn't do much to help Tristan see, rather, it was just a different kind of blindness. But after a few moments, his eyes adjusted and he squinted, stepping forward cautiously.

"I'm here because I have made up my mind. I'm going to get you out of here. I want you to-"

The angel coughed somewhere in the darkness- straight ahead?- and Tristan felt some tension dissipate. At least they hadn't moved it after all. That made things *slightly* easier.

"Angel? Have you heard what I've been saying?"

"Uh huh."

"You have to pray to them, to your friends, like- do whatever it takes to get their attention! Pray using whatever words that will get them over here. Tell them that at…" *What time is it?! I'll just estimate.* "…at 6am, or when the sun rises, you and me will be at the highest parapet of the castle. No matter what, we'll get there, and if they meet us there, they can take you back to your home. After that, I guess it's up to them, but… but we'll be at the top parapet."

"What if they don't come?"

"They're coming." said Tristan. "Trust me, they're coming to destroy the kingdom. But if you like… I don't know, just pray super hard, and like I said, maybe your friends will hear! You can at least get out of here. I can… I can prove that people from Donabela aren't… Well, at any rate, you can get out of here." Tristan knelt and fumbled the key ring in one hand. The match in his other hand was growing short. It would sear his fingertips in a moment. The angel's exhausted eyes took on a dark flare in the flickering light. They were chameleon blue, taking the color of whatever light shone on them.

He looked like he didn't believe him. His eyes were expectant, as if awaiting the inevitable 'gotcha!' But in a moment, the shackles fell from his wrists and feet. The collar was welded on, but the chain was able to be unhooked, and soon fell on the ground as well. As he helped him stand upright, Tristan hoped and prayed- though not to some bloodthirsty god- that the sun hadn't risen already.

***

Listen to me. Before you go back or do anything else, just listen.

My head was spinning when the man helped me walk through that darkness. I kept thinking that he was taking me to my execution. I figured, you know, what with how they typically act, that cruel mind games weren't outside the realm of possibility.

But eventually we came to an area flooded with brightness- well, it was probably actually dim, but to my eyes it was like looking into the sun.

I'm not sure what happened. I was actually warm, and the air felt fresh. I didn't even care anymore about the pain radiating through my whole being.

Then- it became cool again. All this time, I was praying fervently to you, but I have to say, I became hopelessly distracted. Outside, it wasn't so bright, and my eyes adjusted instead of just burning.

We were climbing up a spiral staircase that entwined around a tower. I heard him mutter a curse. I believe that his fellow guards saw us and made assumptions. Assumptions that perhaps he was buying his deliverance from the doomed city.

The sunrise caught my eye. It was so beautiful.

The man shouted "Angels!?"- and he started dragging me along faster. His colleagues must not have known what to do or who to focus on. I know that firearms were shot at us. I recall the moment a bullet tore through the stomach of my friend. He faltered. All of a sudden it was my own scant strength that supported him.

His hot, sticky blood made the steps slippery- we almost fell. But by then, they were firing at you. You remember. It is a blessing that none of you were harmed.

Yes, I understand what they did to me. Nobody knows better than me, so please don't try to explain it to me as if I am unaware.

But they also harmed their own, my friend Tristan. He was the only one who visited me, the only one who treated me with kindness, and the only one who gave me any sort of hope. I do not believe that he was the only one like that in the entire city. And you don't think- you don't really think that one person deserves to die for the crimes of their countrymen, yes?

Well, maybe if they are destroyed again they will continue to become worse. I myself won't stand for snuffing out a civilization that very well might have more good people in it.

We'll never know if we don't give them a chance.

Don't speak to me as if I don't know that. I'm reminded of it every time I see you fly. I feel trapped, shackled. I know that they're the ones who did it to me. But that was… a collective, I suppose. And if an individual can be righteous, I do believe that so can the collective. Eventually.

So long as we give it a chance to grow.

People Who Touch Garbage

It became like a drug, the ability to *see through* did. I can understand why mother always had me wear gloves as a child, and why she didn't want me to end up like *them*. The people who touch garbage. People to feel sorry for, but never to actually help. Of course not, that would require getting close to them.
I remember the day I told mother and father that I could see through- though I didn't realize it was such a phenomenon. I mean, it isn't *rare*, but 47.3% of the population having it does not make it terribly *common*.

It was this penguin statuette on my bedside table. When I was three, I loved that penguin statue. It looked like a normal, cartoony penguin, but it had red hearts painted on its black back and wings.

I picked it up one Saturday to play tea party, and it was like a movie playing before- no, that's not right. Not *before* my eyes. That sounds too passive. It was like I *was* the penguin statuette, experiencing the craftsman at the China shop painting my red hearts. At the same time though, it was like I was the craftsman, the paintbrush, the paint. I felt such love imparted onto me, such satisfaction in having created something. I recalled being placed on the shelf, I recall being purchased, I saw my own face gazing at it in dim lighting as I fell asleep.

Then I was me again, but the feeling lingered. I'd soon come to learn that you can see through the same object as much as you want, but that feeling stayed with you the longest after your first time. I told them, so excitedly, that I had seen the penguin be painted, and that I had been on the shelf being bought, and that I saw myself fall asleep. They knew right away that I was able to see through things. My father has it too, but it's not hereditary it seems. It's just a coincidence.

They explained to me how lovely it was to be able to see through, but that it would be dreadfully distracting to experience it all the time, especially when school started.

A few days later, as more and more objects revealed themselves to me, I was given my first pair of Opaquing gloves. I saw the machine knitting them together, and before that I saw the dyes that made them pink, and before that still I saw the fibers being spun.

Since they were on my hands all the time however, the images and feelings associated with seeing through dulled, and it was like I had never been able to see through.

Indeed, as I got older I took them off and experimented with various objects, but I quickly discovered that there was a reason my mother and father wanted me to wear the gloves.

My mother was preparing chicken, and my seven year old self became immensely curious. I slipped my glove off my right hand and when her back was turned, I pressed on the pale pink raw meat with my index finger.

It was unpleasant to say the least.

To this day, I still can't stomach chicken, and I recall that I didn't try out any new objects for a while after that whole business.

But every night before falling asleep, I let my hand brush against my penguin statuette.

As I got older, I realized and experienced more of the difficulties of being able to see through. I of course, wore my gloves all the time, as there was no way I would make it through a single hour of school without being completely disoriented. I didn't need to see the entire history of a single pencil, or the gum stuck to the underside of my desk. Sometimes kids who could see through would take off their gloves on purpose and touch something really disgusting so that they could be excused from class. If it was too much of a recurring thing with a particular student, they could be suspended or even expelled. I remember that happening sometimes. I never did it, I was too worried about being a bad student.

Once, I got bullied into touching something gross. It wasn't out of genuine malice, I understand now, but at the time it was horrible, and it left quite the negative mark on me as I grew up. I was eight years old, and me and the other girls found a dead lizard. A completely flattened dead lizard, out in the parking lot while we were waiting for our parents to pick us up.

"Do you think a car ran over it?" one of them asked, as we four leaned down around it in a circle. You know how it is with young kids, what disgusts adults morbidly fascinates them.

"Must've been one of the cars."

"Poor little guy."

I spoke last, and suggested burying it.

"Maybe Clara should touch it." I looked up at Lucy in surprise, with my mouth dropping open. I had always considered us friends, but the older I get the more I realize I just *thought* she was my friend. Lucy probably just kept me around because I went along with anything.

"Why should I touch it?" I asked incredulously.

"Clara can see through it, she should touch it."

"But- Hey, c'mon." I said, trying to get myself out of the situation without actual conflict. I really liked Lucy, and I wanted her to keep being my friend.

"Go ahead Clara, don't be a 'fraidy-cat. You aren't a 'fraidy-cat, are you?"

I realized then that there was no getting out of this without making Lucy mad. I grimaced and looked down at the lizard to hide the fact that my eyes were watering a little. I heard Lucy and the other girl- I'm afraid I forgot her name- laughing in anticipation. Then I touched the dead lizard.

Sometimes when I pet my cat, I tasted the nasty canned food as if I was the one who had eaten it, but it was made worth it by experiencing the warm feeling of curling up in the sun and sleeping for hours. The lizard was similar, except instead of feeling like a warm cat in the sun, I felt like it was my own skull being crushed under the tire of a hatchback van.

I was out of school for a few days after that. Lucy acted a little differently toward me after that. We didn't hang out so much. Now that we're adults, I sometimes see her in public and we exchange the typical niceties. I can see in her eyes though, she still remembers the parking lot.

So, does the ability to see through also extend to other people? After finding out that I could see through, I was told that I should never touch people without my gloves on- not unless they were somebody that I was so close to that they wouldn't mind, or even actually want it. Most people who could see through couldn't see through other people until they were older, in their twenties or something. Some people who could see through never saw through another person, even if they got married. It was something about your hands, so if you never wanted to see through another person, you just wore the gloves all the time.

My father always wore his gloves, and I asked him once how he resisted the urge to take them off sometimes. He shrugged and before he went back to reading, he told me that you just sort of got used to it. After a while, you stopped feeling the gloves.

Seeing through another person is intensely intimate, and often unpleasant. I've heard of people who have gone mad after daring to see through another person. You see everything when you touch a person with your hand. All the good things, all the bad things, every secret, every memory. It is the most beautiful and horrifying thing, to experience every part of a person at once- like forcing a camel through the eye of a needle. The "high" as it were, lasts for days, maybe even weeks, but it isn't always a good feeling. I've only seen through three people, and it was enough to knock me off kilter for a month each time. The sense of depersonalization is always a risk when you decide to see through as much as you can, but with people it is so much worse, for both parties.

I had my first kiss at sixteen. Kenneth Ransom. I thought we were going to be together forever. We were of course, very stupid. He let me take my gloves off, and I pressed his face between my hands when I kissed him.

I came to my senses a few weeks later, after a whole month of dreaming through his entire life, dreaming that I *was* Kenneth Ransom. I know more than I ever could want to know about Kenneth Ransom, born in Monterey, California. I can't very easily forget either, not all that vivid detail. I got off lucky, though. Kenneth was- and still is, I suppose- a completely normal guy. He'd never experienced

anything unusually horrific or stressful. If I hadn't
been so lucky, I might very well have gone completely
mad.

It goes without saying that we broke up. It
wasn't as messy as you'd think, but for obvious
reasons we couldn't stay together. I mean, we couldn't
even look at each other afterwards, really.

So it's no wonder then, that sometimes I saw
news stories about people who could see through
cutting off their own hands.

"I just feel so much more free." said this guy
in a hospital gown on the news. The camera
strategically included his bandaged stumps in the shot,
sitting on his lap.

"People might not understand, people might
call me crazy, but now I can finally get on with my
life."

It was that kind of thing that caused them to
hasten the production of a drug.

I remember when that drug first went out on
the market. It's called *tactinyl*, and at the time people
were treating it like it was the second coming- the
solution to every problem relating to seeing through.

My coworker at the cafe, Allison, could also
see through, and she was so excited when the TVs
behind the counter started running another news
story on *tactinyl*.

"Are you going to get it? One tablet every
morning versus gloves all day, no brainer, right?"

"Hmm. Maybe." I said distantly. I had so much trouble focusing on what I was doing sometimes. Especially during slow hours, it was easy for me to space out completely at the counter.

"I mean, I'm definitely going to wait a while before getting a prescription. Something put out so fast, that's kind of risky, isn't it? But still. It's an awesome idea, and I think it'll really solve a lot of problems." she sort of nodded in the direction of the large plate glass window in the front. There was a homeless guy out there, rifling through the garbage. We were supposed to politely ask people like that to leave, but neither me or Allison was ever comfortable doing that.

I thought to myself, those pills won't solve a thing if people who touch garbage can't access them. Who's to say they'd even want them.

"I'll probably wait too. The gloves aren't a big deal for me." I laughed. "My hands get sweaty anyway, I feel a lot better having gloves on so I don't feel like I'm gonna drop everything I hold."

Allison was about to say something else, but a customer came in and we had to stop chatting. She nodded at me and let me take the register. While I was taking the order- a medium organic cold brew with two pumps of vanilla sweetener, almond milk, and caramel drizzle but no whipped cream- Allison changed the channel from the news to sports. A definite step up.

I got a few letters in the mail from some pharmaceutical company, asking if I would be willing to be a beta tester for the drug. I read the first letter pretty carefully, but I ended up throwing it away. After that, I just ignored them completely. I asked Allison about it, and she said she didn't get any letters.

"What did I do to not get one?" I remember her asking me in jest.

It was the same sort of deal with everyone we knew who could see through. A few got the letters, but most didn't. One time when we had the news on at the cafe, I heard them say that the letters were sent out at random.

I stopped getting them after a while of not answering, and then it looked like they were trying new people, because Allison eventually did get her coveted letter. It was a lot like when you aren't invited to a party and are offended, but really you didn't want to go. Allison brought it to work and showed it to me triumphantly before casually throwing it in the same garbage can we throw old coffee filters.

Somebody must've accepted the offer to test the drug though, because a few years later, it had been approved. In the intervening years, I had been offered quite a few jobs based on my ability to see through. Allison, too. The most interesting one was the one that was offered to us by the city police department. We were both offered this position at separate times, and we both said no.

This job was hard to fill, and there had actually been a proposed bill that everyone registered as seeing through who was also mentally fit should do it for six months, but it got struck down. Thank god.

I actually didn't turn it down right away, in fact, I actually went down to the station to be given an orientation. I was the only one there; I don't know what I was expecting. Nobody wanted this job. The only people who took it were the morbidly curious and those desperate for a paycheck after being turned down everywhere else.

It made sense to me- even though I didn't support it- that people would want to make it mandatory. After all, murder weapons and evidence weren't exempt from seeing through.

So I went in that day, and the detective gave me a spiel about what a significant contribution to society I would be making, and how cold cases were a thing of the past, now that seeing through had become more and more common through the decades of the past century. It takes a special kind of person, he told me. And judging by my file that was updated every year as I had my check-up, I was somebody who could handle the strain of such a job. Of course, as I soon learned, they were probably just looking to fill the position and were saying that to everyone.

"It will only be for six months. Once you sign the contract, you're in it for those six months unless you have serious cause to terminate the contract. However, if you feel that you can handle more, you will be given the option to renew. We've had people stay for up to three years." he said at the end. "We're looking forward to hearing from you. Please don't hesitate if you have any questions or concerns."

He must've said that, or variations on it, half a dozen times as he escorted me out of the building.

"You have a ride coming?"

"Of course, don't worry. I'll be in touch."

"That's great to hear, and please don't hesitate to reach out when you are ready."

"Thanks." I sat down and put my headphones in, hoping he would take that as a cue to go back into the building and call the next person in for an interview.

I know that I really shouldn't have my music on so loud, but it's a small vice that I just can't let go of. It definitely makes my already poor spatial awareness even worse, though, seeing as I didn't even notice when somebody else was standing by the end of the bench.

He had his hands in his pockets, and was nervously chewing his lower lip. He must've been too polite to sit down on the bench, but at the same time too awkward to find somewhere else to stand. I took out one earbud.

"Hey, you can sit down." I said. I scooted closer to the end of the bench, so that there was more of a buffer between us as he sat down.

"Thanks." he said, now bouncing his leg as he sat forward on the edge of the wooden seat.

"No prob. You're cool." I said. I was about to put my earbud back in and continue whatever it was I was reading or looking at- I forgot- but he kept talking.

"My name's uh, Milo. I worked at the station back there. Today was my last day. They're looking for a replacement, but I don't think they can find one."

"I was interviewing today, or doing orientation or something."

"Oh yeah?" I saw his eyes flit to my hands, and he saw my gloves. The ones I was wearing that day were pale pink, I remember that much. I was going through a phase where I tried to coordinate the color of my gloves with my clothes.

"Are you uh, are you going to take it?"

I shrugged, as if to say *I dunno*, but in fact, I did know that there was no way I was taking it. I love true crime and me and my dad bonded over watching murder documentaries, but I didn't want to be *this* close to all that.

"You probably shouldn't. Unless it's like, you really need money or something. Cuz like, the money's good, but I don't really think it's worth it. They want me to sign on for another six months, but I keep saying no."

"Mmm." I said, finally resigning to the fact that until the taxi got there, I would either have to pause my music and make conversation or just be a jerk and tell him to fuck off.

"Yeah, I managed to get another job at that uh, that grocery store on Casa Verde. The one that sells little seven dollar things of paprika."

I immediately knew which one he was referring to, even though the street name meant nothing to me- I navigate by landmarks, street names are far beyond me.

"You talking about *Carrie's Pantry*? I found the most expensive chocolate bar ever there one time. Some kind of organic dark chocolate with dried cherries thing, it was six bucks and pretty small." I laughed.

"Yeah. None of the other places I applied to called back. I think that the pantry had its doubts, but I'm pretty chatty, so I think they liked that."
"Being chatty is good. Some customers really like having someone to talk to. I know it's like that at the cafe. Of course, sometimes you get people who are just like, *absolutely not*, and they don't even take out their headphones to order!"

"You work at a cafe?"

I nodded.

"Yeah, the *Wired Bean*. I've been there for ages."

"That's really cool. I should go sometime. I love coffee, it makes me too jittery, but I drink it anyway."

"Have any today?" I sort of chuckled, glancing at his bouncing knee. It was kind of shaking the bench.

"You know it." he must've gotten kind of self conscious, because he stopped bouncing his leg. I saw a taxi coming, and didn't want to end the conversation on an uncomfortable note, but I couldn't think of anything else to say aside from a trite *nice* in response.

"You have a ride coming?" I asked, standing up and making sure I had everything- even though my purse and my phone were both on me, and they were all I had brought.

Milo nodded.

"Yeah, I've got a buddy coming to pick me up."

"Awesome." The taxi pulled up in front of the bench, and I think I awkwardly said *bye* before getting into the back seat. As we were driving away, I realized that I'd never told Milo my name. He was nice enough, if a little odd. Thinking back, I actually enjoyed that exchange on the bench.

Milo came to the 'bean a week or two later. When he saw me, he actually stepped backward like he was going to leave, but I waved him in.

"Hi, Milo." I shouted over the acoustic guitar music that the manager didn't let us turn down. He seemed a little skittish, like a stray cat that you invited into your house to feed. When it was his turn to order, he kept messing up, stammering and mixing up his words, that kind of thing. I probably sound like a jerk, but I laughed. I think that might've been what broke the ice, though.

I won't walk you through the many, many times Milo came to the 'bean and ordered the same drink, because it happened frequently. He started ordering two drinks, and one was for me. I wondered which wing-man friend gave him that tip.

One day, I borrowed the manager's swipe card so I could order something with my employee discount. Once, for fun, I saw through that card. Nothing exciting. I did learn that the manager washes her hands three times after using the bathroom, so I at least get some peace of mind about what germs I'm picking up when I borrow it.

"Watch this, Allison, that guy Milo is gonna come in at a little past four."

"Is that why you're getting the drink? Is it for him?" she asked, spraying whipped cream on the top of a peppermint hot chocolate. It was a rainy December afternoon, after all. We had an unusual number of kids with their parents getting away from the rain.

"Yeah, he always orders this one. Sometimes he buys me a coffee, so I thought I'd return the favor."

The 'bean's prices are pretty high, and the large iced coffee came out to around six dollars. The look on Milo's face was worth it, though. He was nothing short of delighted, and that made me delighted.

He stuck around that afternoon, until my shift was over. I'd told him to stick around. I think that was the day I asked him if he wanted to catch a movie at some point. It actually happened that night. I don't remember what the movie was. There wasn't anything good playing, so we just picked something that looked entertaining. We spent the whole movie making fun of the acting, the special effects, and the plot holes. I remember that it was about a woman who saw through her husband on their wedding night, only to discover that he was a vampire who had been alive and marrying different women for a thousand years. It was based on some young adult novel I'd never read.

Milo's laugh was infectious. I think the rows behind us were annoyed, because the two of us laughed at everything that happened in that stupid movie.

Wasn't bad for a first date, all things considered.

We'd been going out 'officially' for around six months when I took a walk with him down to the pharmacy to pick up his medications. It was a nice- if windy- day, and he was chattering nonstop as we walked.

I was still drunk on being in a relationship- the first one I'd had since highschool- but I was starting to want to learn more about him. More specifically, I wanted to know more of the, well, not necessarily the *bad*. It would be more accurate to say that I wanted to know the worst as well as the best. I really liked this guy, and I wanted to be sure that he was someone I could continue really liking. Before things went on too long, you know.

Milo never wore gloves. I didn't ask about it, since I knew it was considered a bit of a faux pas to ask if someone was taking *tactinyl*. But that day, when

I asked if I could go walking with him and he said yes,
I saw it included in the trio of medications he picked
up from the window. I recognized an antidepressant,
as well.

He chuckled nervously, and stuffed them into
his messenger bag.

"Store bought neurotransmitters, am I right?"

I was taught to never laugh at things like that,
that matters of mental health were no place for jokes-
just like car crashes and cancer-, but I laughed and
said "that's funny". I was starting to learn that if you
couldn't laugh at things, it would be that much harder
to cope with them. Learning nuance and discretion is
one of the hardest things about getting older.

"I'm not crazy or anything like that." said
Milo, apparently under the impression that I thought
depression was equal to 'crazy' supervillains in a
movie.

"Oh yeah, I know that. I mean, it's no
different from having an inhaler or something."

"Yeah." he said, as we rounded a corner. This
street had a lot of restaurants. I was planning on
surprising him with sushi. My tips had been good that
week, I felt like William Randolph Hearst.

I was about to propose my plan, when he
stopped in the street near a garbage bin with a
cigarette tray on the top.

"My mom like, wasn't that great." he blurted,
as if he'd been holding his breath and just now was
exhaling. I think I tried and failed to respond around
three times. The way I see it, the sidewalk isn't exactly
the best place to crack out the mommy issues.

"Uh, oh, I'm- I'm sorry about that. That sucks."

"Yeah, I had a problem with doing this for a while-" he mimed reaching into the garbage can. "When I was a little kid. Because she was always on meth and stuff."

"That's awful."

"And like, sometimes I miss it, being all-" he waved his hand around above his head "-you know, all the time. It's hard to go back to real life after being zoned out for so long. Even when you come to and you suddenly have really nice adopted parents, and nice brothers and sisters, and they actually make you dinner and make sure you get to school and stuff."

I couldn't think of anything reassuring or nice to say. Everything was either too generic (I'm so sorry) or too social-media-fake-positivity (Thank you for being so vulnerable with me). I just took his hand and nodded at the sushi place.

"Wanna eat something? My treat."

Don't think that I completely shut him down about that. At the moment, I couldn't think of anything to say, but eventually- maybe four California rolls later- I did say something.

"You're pretty awesome, you know."

"Huh?" His mouth was full.

"I was awkward earlier. I've never been through anything like that, so I didn't know what to say. But I think you're awesome, because you're always so cheerful, even though you have a lot of reasons not to be. Oh, not like your life sucks or anything, I didn't mean that, I just mean that there's a lot of people who've been through less than you, but they decide that means it's okay for them to be assholes. I like that you choose to be funny instead."

Milo shrugged. He was tapping his fingers on the table nervously, but he was also smiling. I wondered if I had gone too far. I didn't want to make him feel like he was up on a pedestal or had any crazy high standards to live up to.

"So, we're okay? You don't think there's any sort of issue that would make things not uh, not work out?"

I shook my head. I wasn't ready to commit yet, but if we broke up in the future, I was sure it wouldn't be because he took antidepressants.

"How's the book going? The one I recommended?" I asked, hoping that my subject change wasn't too abrupt.

"It's good. You really weren't kidding about it being different from the movie."

"Which do you like better?"

He thought for a moment.

"You know, they're both weird." he said. "But in different ways. I think the movie definitely went for a more heartwarming approach, and the book has more dark humor..." Once I got him started about the book versus the movie, he kept on talking for ages, and I swear, it was just as entertaining as the book and movie themselves.

Despite her earlier enthusiasm about the drug, Allison never actually got a prescription for *tactinyl*. Neither did I. We both felt validated in our decision when a news story came on the TV at the 'bean, all about how a small percentage of users suffered blood clots. It wasn't exactly shocking news. The drug had been out for two years, and blood clots were a well known side effect. I suppose the body count had finally gotten high enough for the news to care.

"I know it's a small percentage, but 300 people nationwide *dead?* I don't like that." she said, shaking her head.

I adjusted the ring on my finger, slid over my glove. We'd gotten it a size bigger just so I could wear it and my gloves at the same time.

"Cue the conspiracy theorists saying it's a plot to wipe out seeing through people."

"Don't give them ideas." Allison chortled. I was roommates with Allison at the time, and neither of us watched the news. I mean, we weren't *ignorant*, at least not on purpose. Life just reaches a point where you've got too much going on to consider spending free time learning about all the shit making the world worse. Pretty much the only time we actually watched TV news was when we were at work, and a lot of the time we changed the channel to something else, like that channel that shows nonstop cat and dog training reality shows.

I'm not really surprised then, that neither of us really noticed when apparently the death toll started to spike suddenly, three years after the release of the drug.

We got married. A small thing, not a big deal. Neither of us wanted anything seriously fancy or expensive. Afterwards, we drove all the way up to this town called Blue Moon Bay. It was one of those tiny coastal towns populated with cutesy boutiques and pricey coffee shops. A total hotspot for weekend couple's getaways. We didn't stay in the most expensive bed and breakfast, but it was still really nice. At the time, so far as I was concerned, I would've been fine with a barn, so long as it meant that I was with Milo.

The only thing weighing hard on my mind though, was gloves.

Whenever I brought it up, whether or not I should wear gloves when we had sex, he waffled around for a while before saying something noncommittal like, "you should do whatever you want to do".

As we were driving up there, I made my decision. He was on the drug, and couldn't see through. It wouldn't really be fair if I saw through him and he didn't get to see through me. He didn't question when the gloves didn't come off, either. I suppose he was a bit distracted at the moment.

The next morning, we were walking on the beach with our shoes off, eating saltwater taffy out of a brown paper bag.

"I should touch this." I said, holding up a pink glob. "Find out what it's like to get stretched on one of those hooks."

Milo shuddered.

"Ugh, don't say that. Just thinking about it makes me feel weird."

"I think it would be fun to know what it's like to be a piece of taffy."

Milo kicked a piece of seaweed. I wanted him to laugh and joke around like usual, but he was quiet that day. Sometimes he just had quiet days, and that was okay.

"You might be the only person who has ever said that. Now me, if I wasn't on the thing, I'd want to see through something cool, like…"

"A tiger?"

"Maybe a tiger, yeah. That police station put me off seeing through stuff for fun, though."

"Yeah…" I said. We'd come to a stop. There were otters out a ways, and we were craning our necks for a better look.

"You can see through me if you want, though. I don't mind. I think-" he cleared his throat. I think the wind made his throat dry. "I'd be okay if you wanted to. Do you think it's better or worse for us to know each other *really* well?"

I leaned on him. He was tall, and my head was just at shoulder height.

"I can take anything. Good, bad, you name it."

I can't recount it. Anything else, I'd be fine with. I know that at the time I said that I could handle good, bad, anything- but the me from that afternoon and the me from that evening are two completely different people.

It felt like I blinked, and then there I was, in an ER waiting room in some city between Blue Moon Bay and my own.

He'd been driving, and then he just slumped over at the wheel. We hit a tree. All I needed were stitches on my forehead.

"Ms. Liebermann?" the doctor said, muffled as if through frosted glass. There wasn't anything between us, but I was a million miles away.

"Ms. Liebermann, I need an answer from you. When did your husband start taking *tactinyl*?"

"Oh. He started taking it when it first came out."

"Before they adjusted the formula?"

"I guess so."

"Okay." he said, clicking his pen and pocketing it. He put the clipboard under his arm. "I suppose that could be one possible cause for your husband's stroke. We won't know for sure without more tests. Do you have any place to stay tonight?"

"Can I stay here?"

"Are you sure?"

"Don't have a car at the moment." I almost laughed- wasn't it obvious?

"I can call you a taxi, or maybe one of your family members can come pick you up? I believe it would be best for you to sleep in a hotel or something tonight. Then you can come back tomorrow when we figure out what to do next."

Shaking my head, I stood up out of the uncomfortable waiting room chair.

"I can stay."

Milo was in fragile condition, so they just kept him in that hospital for a while. Allison drove the hour there, and my dad came one day too. He gave me money for the hotel, and said I should come stay with him and mom. I said I'd think about it.

They told me that when they got us to the hospital, Milo was clinically dead. They resuscitated him and spent much of the night trying to figure out what happened to him that made him lose consciousness. People don't usually get strokes when they're 28 years old.

Three nights in a row, I slept in that uncomfortable chair, with its vinyl seat and back, and thin metal armrests- all a soothing shade of teal. I started to hate the painting up in the corner, with its insipid looking angel next to her stupid vase of flowers.

My last memory of Milo is this.
It was maybe around noon, and light was gently streaming into the room through the window. The blinds sliced the sunlight into stripes, and they were dancing across the hills of his legs under the blanket. He breathed peacefully, but only because he was on oxygen. I wish I could say that he looked like he was just sleeping. He was hooked up to too many

machines and he was too pale, with swollen eyes and cheeks. A chunk of his blond hair was shaved off, and in that spot was a surgical incision with purple and yellow edges, stapled shut.

They couldn't wake him up. Not even the surgery they tried did much, if any good. Sure, the blockage was gone. But the damage it had left was irreversible, they said. As soon as his foster parents arrived, they were going to take him off life support.

I was okay with that. He'd already died back in the car, so far as I was concerned. The funny thing is, I was feeling so much, but I couldn't show it. I think the doctors were a little taken aback, but then again, they saw this every day. Normal reactions probably ranged from completely numb to hysterics on the floor. At least, that's what TV taught me. I never had to deal with people dying before, except for a grandparent when I was five and didn't understand.

I pulled my chair close to his bed, and I saw that my hands were shaking, the bubbling up of all my grief trapped inside. Why couldn't I cry? I still don't know.

I rested my hand on his arm. Gloved, of course. I didn't even hear the beeping of the heart monitor or the vague chatter from outside in the hallway. As it had always been since the first dinner and a movie, it was just the two of us. Nothing else in the world mattered.

Now my memory gets fuzzy. I know that I did something very stupid, because I woke up in a hospital bed a month later.

I saw through Milo, and that was when the next year's downward spiral started. I would've been okay, maybe, if it had just been Milo dying. But I saw through him. Why did I do that?

I was a small child, curled up in a nest of toys, food containers, and trash. I loved to see through them all. There was this one candy wrapper that I loved to see through. I had eaten the actual candy a long time ago- when mommy was well enough to buy me something to eat. Sometimes when she was in a bad mood, she kicked me, or threw me against the wall. I still can't move that arm right. When it was too scary, I would see through anything I could get my hands on. Seeing through an empty soda can felt so much better than hiding from mommy when she was angry. Sometimes when I was seeing through, she would shake me and scream at me. I could hear her, but I couldn't come up out of the trance I was in.

One day, I stopped waking up in my dirty little room. I was everything and nothing at once- I was a soda can, I was a popcorn kernel, I was my favorite picture book.

Then I woke up and I was somewhere else, and I never saw mommy again.

There were new people, and they loved me. They put gloves on me and took me to a nice lady who helped me not want to float off in my head anymore. I didn't see through things much anymore, at least for a while. Then I got older, and I gave into the temptation more and more often. There was a support group. I met a girl there, but it didn't work out. I never even stood a chance.

The group helped, but once I moved away for school, it felt like it had never even done me any good. I had to drop out.

Going from job to job to job for several years. My new family-

(Why do I still call them my *new* family?)

-still gave me a place to stay when I got kicked out of my apartment. But I just couldn't stop seeing through things.

Then mom gave me a flier. Help wanted, just go to the police station and prove you can see through.

I saw things I want to unsee. It made me never want to see through again. More effective than a therapist, more effective than a support group with coffee and donuts.

I beta tested that drug, and I got a prescription when it was finally released.

I had my shit together, at least. I applied for a job, and I got it. I met a girl. At first it was just one of those one off encounters. But for me, everything good that's ever happened was unexpected. Somehow, that stupid meeting at the bench where I talked her ear off became a night on a pier.

Fireworks exploding over the ocean in brilliant, multicolored flowers. It was so beautiful that when everything turned dark, I still saw them. Fireworks behind my eyes. Colors bursting and blinking away in just a fraction of a second.

And then, absolutely nothing. Nothing left on this side, at least.

But oh, it was suffocating. The blank emptiness strangled me and forced me awake and I realized that I was not Milo Liebermann. I was just me.

And Milo Liebermann had been buried two weeks ago.

It's all a blur, I must confess. I had to go home and sort through all his stuff, or what remained of his stuff. His family had been let in so they could get his clothes for the funeral.

I remember that I started touching everything. It was never enough. The first night, I fell asleep clinging to an old sweater. He'd worn this sweater almost every day. There was so much warm feeling in that green, knit sweater.

For a while, it was never enough. Then it was too much. I didn't want to remember Milo anymore, I was so tired and I couldn't be sad anymore. Everything in the house however, had some connection to him. So after several weeks of barely stepping outside, I left the house.

The library. I cried with happiness when I saw through a children's book. It had made so many people smile, there were so many sweet memories and feelings attached to that book. I spent so much time there, and it was a relief.

When the library closed, I couldn't go home. I think I found a pawn shop. I touched an old string of pearls, and the associated memories hurt.

I think they kicked me out.

I don't remember anything from then. There's a few threads here and there, but really all I know is stuff that other people have told me.

I remember grabbing anything I could. I forgot about him, and all I knew was the beautiful neutral feeling that came from passively observing tiny fragments of other people's lives. A lollipop wrapper showed me the smile of a child forgetting all about the unpleasant shots he had to get at the doctors just a few minutes earlier. A discarded hiking boot at the dump showed me a man who loved nature walks, and would drive for hours until he was so far away that there wasn't cell reception for twenty minutes in any direction.

A poor plastic doll who was missing her head showed me a girl who outgrew her. I was loved unconditionally. Before that, I was in a box looking out upon the toy aisle in a store. Before that still, I was molten plastic being poured into a mold.

I forgot who I was. I forgot who I was, and it was nice.

Allison was the one who found me and took me back to her apartment. It had been three weeks since I had gone missing. She says that I was digging around in a dumpster behind some restaurant.

My parents wanted me to move back in with them. Maybe I should've. But after a week of sleeping on Allison's couch every night, I promised them I'd see a therapist. I made good on that promise, too.

"Thanks for putting up with me."

She shrugged, stirring ramen noodles into boiling water.

"Don't even mention it. You covered too many of my shifts to count, so don't even mention it."

"You think they'd take me back?"

"I'll put in a good word for you with the manager. *Oh wait*, that's me now."

I smiled for the first time in a while. I had the sudden urge to touch the handle of the pot. I wanted to experience all the food that had been cooked inside it, and I wanted to feel the hunger, anticipation, and all the feelings of the one cooking- good or bad, hurried or not.

Instead, I counted to five, and I kept my gloves on.

The only thing I've touched since then is my penguin statue. It still makes me happy, and every day only adds new memories. The therapist suggested having a "safe" object, and I couldn't think of anything better than my penguin statue.

Sometimes I feel like I'll never stop being a loser working at a coffee shop. But I get to work with my best friend, and that's not something that a lot of people can say.

I'm luckier than most people. I try to remember that when I start feeling sorry for myself, or when I see homeless people touching garbage outside the 'bean. I'm lucky that I had an Allison to help me when I lost my Milo.

I hope that someday it won't hurt to think of his name.

But over all, the world keeps turning, and it is treating me better now.

Some days though, I do admit. It would be easier to just touch garbage and forget myself. Forget myself and float away.

William Hoyle's Shop of Arcana

"You know how some people are allergic to bee stings? This is sort of the same thing." I say, replacing the bandage on the young man's neck. He lies on the makeshift examination bed, located in the small room behind my shop's counter. When mundane medicine can't help, the back room of a magic shop works in a pinch, after all.

"So, what, he's allergic to vampire bites?" asks one of his three hovering friends.

"Mmm-hmm! Pretty much." I say, pulling open a drawer from the tall, wooden shelf where I keep various potions, herbs, and crystals. Just basic things for healing. These kids are pretty damn lucky I don't have to take eight hours to brew some obscure potion. I scoop a few spoonfuls of dried, crushed flower petals into a little bag. I hand it to the brown haired hovering girl with a ponytail.

"What's that for?" asks the guy standing in the corner, arms folded.

"So, you're going to brew up some hot water and- do you have a tea strainer?- brew it up like tea, and have him drink it once a day right before bed. You guys are college students, right?"

"Yeah, Pacific Conservatory." says the girl in a green sweater with yellow polka dots.

"He have a roommate?"

"Yeah, I'm his roommate." says the guy.

"Then it's your responsibility, here." I toss him a small, silver object. "Tea strainer."

The guy looks a little confused, holding it up by the hook that goes on the edge of the cup. He's pinching it between his thumb and forefinger like he's afraid it'll bite or something.

"How do I use this?"

Ah, must be a coffee drinker.

"Just put a tablespoon of petals in it, and plop the whole thing in the water."

"Oh, okay."

"Wait, so has the uh, lady been getting him every night?" the ponytail girl asks. "Don't they need to be invited in? How's he still sick?"

"He's just having a nasty reaction to the one bite." I pat the young man's shoulder. He blinks awake, shivering from fever. I'm not sure he's entirely aware of where he is.

"The ER just said he had a really bad flu. Then Fiona started doing all this research, after all the weird stuff we saw…" says ponytail girl.

"Well, kudos for Fiona." I say. "He's got competent friends, even if he himself is kinda dumb and horny." I nudge the young man jokingly. He doesn't register what I say, but I know he'll be more lucid as soon as he has some of my tea mix. His friends are a little offended though.

"Hey, Dante isn't like that." says Fiona. "You yourself said that these creatures are really seductive."

"Yeah, seriously, it wasn't his fault." The roommate adds.

"Ay, remind me not to wander off during gigs." he slurs, ponytail girl and the roommate helping him up off my examination table.

"Oh yeah, of course. But, next time you get a late night gig at a fancy house, wear a crucifix or eat a lot of garlic before. Or just don't take a gig from vampires." I say, opening the back-room door.

"Well, it's not like we *knew*." says Fiona. "But thanks, Mr. Hoyle."

"Any time. Hop on into my shop again when you guys are all nice and *not* chewed on."

I sit down behind the counter after holding the door for them.

They were nice kids, and I'm pretty jazzed to get a case with a happy ending. Provided the roommate follows the instructions I wrote down for him.

I put my feet up on the glass case counter. I know, it's not good manners, but it's my shop, and there aren't any customers in anyway. Business can be slow, but people like those kids pay me pretty well. It's worth it, considering that a regular-ass doctor can't help everyone.

I sit, and before folding them behind my head, I clap my hands to make a nearby record playing start playing *Petrouchka.*

I tell people it's motion activated.

All the little trinkets and antiques are in some way enchanted, but I find a playful way to explain it away or minimize it.

Just the right amount of explainable magic charms people. Too much, and it freaks them out.

"Oh, this ring- they say it increases your appeal- that it brings love!"

That's true, it brings out a person's beautiful features while minimizing flaws.

"This scarf is made of alpaca wool, it's extremely warm."

It's a Helios Scarf- it radiates a gentle heat.

"This music box plays *It's Only a Paper Moon.* It's the perfect baptism present for your nephew." It's been enchanted to make babies fall asleep. I think to myself, I should do something productive. I polish a few silver lockets I have in the jewelry case, and I go re-alphabetize the used books that people browsing mixed up. Then I wipe down the glass in the cursed objects case. I don't have this in the main room. I use the basement as a sub-room for expensive and other items I don't want on public display. I have this case there, and other cursed items that cost me a pretty penny.

This is a nice case. Dark oak wood, thankfully *not* cursed. I heard once of an arcana shop owner who thought it would be *cool* to keep a cursed trumpet in a cursed glass box. Yeah, he's not around anymore.

I don't really sell this stuff, at least, I haven't in a while.

I like showing people the items. It's a good show, and it makes people want to buy things.

I have an old mirror that's said to show hallucinations in the reflection, like a dead body on the floor, or a bat about to bite you. That's the most harmless of the cursed objects, and far from the worst mirror I've ever had. What is it about mirrors that makes people want to jinx them?

As I'm staring at a cologne that causes erectile dysfunction, I hear the bell at my front door jingle, heralding a customer.

"Oh, be right up there!" I shout, tossing the cleaning rag over my shoulder and picking up my spray bottle.

I tug back the curtain as I reach the top of the short stairs, just in time to see the door swing shut.

I put the cleaning stuff on the glass counter display case, craning my neck to get a look at the customer.

"Welcome! Anything in particular I can help you find?" I can't get a clear view of them- they're behind a shelf housing a selection of chinaware.

"Let me know if I can help you find anything." I say when they don't answer. Sometimes they don't. I mean, maybe they have headphones in, or maybe they just don't want to say hi. Who wouldn't want to say hi to me? Coward.

I start browsing my own shelves, just to look like I'm doing something.

And yeah, to get a look at the guest. It feels weird to not know who's skulking around in my own shop.

They've started browsing the used books, their back to me. All I can see is that they're wearing a black hoodie with the hood up.

The used books are set up in kind of an open-ended rectangle of shelves, making a nook. There's no way I can get a better look at them, so I go back to the counter. I decide to polish some more jewelry. Always look busy. Somehow it makes your business look livelier.

"Hey- the sign up front says that paperbacks are three for five bucks. That apply to those editions with like… flexible leather covers?"

"Oh! Uh, sure, why not." I say, walking back up to the counter and narrowly avoiding tripping on a rocking horse that somehow has escaped from the toy section. I swear that little fucker can move on its own.

The guest doesn't say anything for the moment. I suppose he's gone back to browsing.

"The books aren't cursed, right?"

"Huh?" I laugh. "No, I keep the cursed books in the basement along with the evil dolls. I say, half joking.

"And those aren't for sale?"

I hear him walking around, to the row of old clocks and jewelry boxes this time.

"Nah. It's more of a mini museum of curiosities. Admission is five bucks if you're interested."

"Do you have a Fiji mermaid?"

He's almost in view. I catch a glimpse of him walking past antique wind-up toys. He too almost trips on the rocking horse. Maybe it *should* be down in the basement.

"You should have a Fiji mermaid. Or something like it. People like to look at dead shit."

"I'll uh, consider it."

"At any rate, that's more fun than a necklace that strangles the wearer, right?"

I raise my eyebrows and go back to polishing my own fingerprints off the glass.

"You've heard of the Onegin Sapphire?" I have a necklace with a shrinking chain that's killed eight people.

"Yeah. Be honest, if someone offered you enough, would you sell it to them?"

"I uh, well, no?" I mean, sometimes I sell under the table to exorcists, but only because they can destroy some cursed artifacts. Otherwise, they really *are* safer with me, even if they're being used for cheap entertainment.

"Selling a cursed object would be pretty irresponsible, right?"

"Yep." I say. "Irresponsible."

The customer rounds a corner and approaches the counter. He's got a surgical mask on, but I can still tell his face is covered in a myriad of scars in a bizarre pattern, sort of like when a window gets broken. He's got two paperbacks and one faux leather book, clutched in his arms.

"Can I check out the back? I'd like to see the curiosities." he says, reaching with one hand into his pocket and putting a five on the glass counter.

"Sure." I say. I feel a little odd taking this guy out back. He's oddly confrontational. Was he from the same church as those evangelicals who thought I was devil worshipper?

I pull back the curtain and make a *you first* gesture like the good host I am.

"Pretty small for a museum." says the young man when he reaches the bottom of the stairs. I feel a little insulted. I worked hard to furnish this room to look like the spooky fortune teller tent at a carnival, and I would appreciate some positive feedback.

"Well, you know. Adds to the charm. Makes it feel more creepy. Really pulls in the foot traffic during October."

He makes a noncommittal grunt.

"What's this?" he points to a violin in a locked glass case.

"That's the uh, Donizetti Violin. Made in 1765. Very nice make, but the craftsman was cursed by his mistress when he wouldn't leave his wife. Any instrument he made would deafen the listener. I'm talking eardrums bursting, full on-" I make a *pssshh* noise and mime blood bursting out of my ears.

The man laughs weakly and drifts over to a cabinet with a padlock on it.

"What's in here?"

"Oh, not much." I say. I take out a skeleton key. I twirl it around on my index finger theatrically.

"Only the most cursed painting on the west coast!"

"Whoa. Should you even open the cabinet then? It's it irresponsible to keep it on display?"

I shake my head and start to unlock it. The lock is a little stubborn.

"It's only dangerous if you look at it too long. It's the eyes of the crying lady. Her weeping face is so pathetic that first- within thirty seconds- the observer starts to cry. Then, the observer turns hysterical, manic, psychotic, whatever. After just a minute, the damage is irreparable." I pause before opening the cabinet as I always do- hands dramatically pressed on the crease between the doors, as if holding something back. I take a deep breath. Showmanship is everything- since obviously I can't actually let anyone get cursed. It all falls on me, and to be honest, I quite enjoy it.

"Once the damage is done, the poor soul must be permanently restrained, or else they'll just hurt themselves until, well, y'know… So…" I turn around ominously, one hand still on the wood.

"Do you care to take a look? Ten seconds? Fifteen? How long will you risk it?"
The man is- I guess predictably- unimpressed. I don't know why I even put on the full show for him.

"Do whatever. I don't know who's dumber. The PT Barnum who risks his guests' lives, or the morons who fall for it."

I drop the drama and lock the cabinet.

"Okay then. To be fair, you *did* ask to see the museum."

He doubles over, clapping his hand over his masked mouth. He has one of those laughs that's silent at first, then high and brittle sounding. Almost like a creaking hinge.

"Um…"

"No, no, go ahead, unlock it. Please, unlock it. I'm not here to rain on your parade!" as he continues to creak, I stiffly turn back around, and I fight with the lock again.

"Sticky lock, huh?" he says, having finally caught his breath.

"Yep." I say flatly.

As soon as I get it unlocked, I feel something crack over my head. Before I hit the floor, I think to myself, I hope he didn't just break something expensive.

***

I come to, and my head is throbbing. As everything slides into focus, I realize that I'm still in the museum. Yeah… in the museum, and tied to a chair.

Before I even realize it, I'm struggling. I can see the busted ceramic jar on the ground, and I suppose it's that old Salem Witch's ashes that are all over my shoulders right now.

That little bastard is rifling through the cabinets, reading the information cards, and putting them back as if shopping for just the right item.

"A ring that causes nausea. Nahh… Oh, here we go." he rises to his feet with a pocket watch. "A pocket watch that can freeze a person in time for the duration set. I think this is a bit too powerful to be sitting around in some guy's shop. I mean, a cat burglar could just waltz right in and snatch it. That's not cool."

I try to talk, but my head is spinning. If I open my mouth, I might just throw up. Whatever, though. I've been through worse. So what if he steals my stuff? He doesn't know how to handle any of it, so he'll probably be dead, incapacitated, or insane by the end of the day.

"Of course, I don't think you're too concerned about that." He pulls his mask down, revealing the full extent of the 'cracks' on his face.

"After you sold me that mirror for my dorm, my roommate got drunk one night and broke it. My face was reflected in it when he threw the textbook, and just like that! Blood everywhere. Same pattern as the break."

Oh shit.

"I did some digging around, after I got out of the hospital. Nobody would believe me when I said it had to be the mirror. But hoo-boy, I knew as soon as I found out about other incidents involving people who bought stuff from you."

"I don't- I don't sell this stuff anymore." A sour taste is in my mouth. He's not here to rob me.

"Hell yeah, you don't! The operative word of course being *anymore!*" He throws the pocket watch against the wall, and I flinch as it goes sailing over my head before shattering.

"But before you learned your lesson, people had to get hurt. Was it worth the money?"

"Look- it was wrong. Really wrong, and I shouldn't have ever done that. I just… I didn't think anything so bad would… would happen."

I chose items that I didn't think would do any serious harm. Also, I just used to suck at judging the nature of an enchantment. It was careless and stupid, but so much time had passed- well, three years- and I figured nothing seriously bad had happened.

"I thought, I thought, I thought," he says in a sing-song voice. "I almost bled to death while your pockets got lined! The nerves in my face got slashed to bits, I had to learn how to *eat* again! Do you want to know about what happened to all the other people? Other people you ruined?"

I honestly don't. I uh, honestly *don't.* Watching this guy accidentally drool on himself while talking is hard enough to watch, knowing that it's all because I sold him a cursed mirror for his dorm.

"I'll tell you what happens next. You're going to sit very still, and be very quiet, and listen to every story I found of something bad happening to someone because of you." he browses the cabinet I was polishing earlier, wiping his mouth. He reaches through the shattered glass and takes out a tiny dessert plate with a clear cloche on it. There are two delicate, powder-coated cookies on it. I hope he doesn't see my eyes widen.

"What's this? Stale old cookies?" he reads the card that had sat next to them in the case. "Marionette Cookies. Tell me about these. C'mon, give me what I paid for." he takes the cloche off, and hovers the plate under my nose. I shudder to think about what would happen if I inhale any of the powdered sugar, even though I've already inhaled Salem Witch ashes.

"Um…"

"C'mon! The story behind these ratty old cookies!"

"Okay, okay! Marionette Cookies. In 1896, the nanny Lizaveta Andreiovna crafted these with the intention of quieting down the annoying children she was looking after. She included a pinch of sawdust from a puppet that had been retired from the Shrovetide fair that year, some busted up old clown thing."

"Ah, hope that didn't wreck the flavor." he says, picking one up and looking at it. It's a little too close to my nose.

"Y-yeah, I know, right? Anyway, the ending's predictable, the kids ate the cookies, got turned into wooden marionettes forever, the remaining two cookies got passed around and are a hot item for arcana shops and curiosity museums to get. You don't wanna know how much those stale cookies cost me." I try to laugh. Always laugh, maybe it'll make your kidnapper laugh and let you go.

"Wow. Too bad you couldn't get a hold of the little kid puppets." says the man, uncomfortably close to my face. He bumps the tip of my nose with the cookie.

"C'mon, man. A little- a little disproportionate, you think-!" he drops the plate, and with one hand pinches my nose while the other shoves the cookie in my mouth.

I'm kicking him, I'm desperately trying to wrench my hands free, but I can't. It dawns on me just now that I've never been in a corner *this* bad.

I swear to God I'm struggling as hard as I possibly can, but eventually my brain decides it would rather take its chance with a cursed cookie than suffocate, and I reflexively swallow.

At first, there's nothing but the relief that I can breathe again.

Then my back starts to hurt. I'm forced to sit up straight, and I watch as the skin on my arms hardens and the joints crack out- it would be agony if the feeling hadn't vanished from my limbs already. I'm screaming, but I'm choked into silence as the wooden texture spreads to my neck, and then my face freezes too.

Oh my god, it won't stop.

Only my eyes can move, and I see the young man, powdered sugar down the front of his hoodie from the struggle, backing away slowly with a look of horror on his face. He runs away, and I hear him tripping up the stairs.

I'm completely numb, and for a moment breathing is difficult as my insides are squeezed. That's not a problem for long though, because now I don't *have* to breathe- but I still feel like I'm suffocating.

So tight and stiff, and I'm waiting for it to be over, but I realize that it *is* done- this is just what it feels like to be a curiosity in my own shop.

Flashlight Story

There's a river in my town that nourishes the roots of a great tree. It's from this tree that a man once hung himself- at least that's what the stories say.

So many times I heard that story, in bedsheet tents with flashlights under chin. Each retelling is a little different, every time a little more gruesome. In one version, the over-enthusiastic narrator declared that the pressure of the rope ripped his head clean off. In a pinch, it would do. My friend Barbara had a big brother who could sometimes sneak us into spooky movies, but most of the time we had to get our fix from urban legends and stuff. Overall, they were good stories.

But I could never just let a story be a story.

I wondered if it was true, or rather, which *version* was true. Some of them were really out there, saying that he was possessed by the devil and sacrificed his wife, and when he came to his senses, he hung himself out of remorse and shame. One other version said he was killed by an angry mob after he murdered a little girl. Other versions said that he just got rejected by the woman he was in love with. For whatever reason, I never considered the possibility that there *was* no hanging man.

I went to the library for a start, looking at crumbling old newspapers. It was hard to discern the year of the story. Sometimes the stories said the early 1900s, some said the 30s, and others said it was as recent as 1965, which, coincidentally, is the year I was born in. So naturally, I started there.

My system wasn't a very efficient one, and I eventually had to overcome my shyness and ask the librarian for some help.

"The hanging tree? That's an urban legend, just like the old haunted saw mill. I doubt anyone ever actually died there. I'll take a look at the newspaper archives if you want to be sure, though." she said, upon seeing the note of disappointment in my face.

She didn't find anything. There was no evidence that a man was ever hung from that tree. There was however, one interesting thing. A rather sad one.

The librarian brought up that near the tree, a woman named Anne Weber *did* die an accidental death by falling into the river and hitting her head, then drowning.

I wondered if there was some connection between that death, back in 1904, and the story we told slumber parties in 1979.

After school one afternoon in March, with my polaroid camera case slung over my shoulder, I rode my bike to the hanging tree next to the river in the forest. It rained frequently that week, and the river was a little swollen, and tumbling over the rocks and fallen trees in a rush of furious foam. The river was so swollen up that crossing it to get to the old abandoned saw mill would be next to impossible.

There was nothing, of course, to indicate that someone had died there. The roar of the river was mesmerizing though, and I sat down on a rock to watch. Staring at the water was something I had a hard time pulling myself away from.

I looked up at the hanging tree, the strongest and oldest looking of the trees. I ran my hand along the bark, and traced with my finger the carvings of initials left by couples.
One of them caught my attention, as it was very deep into the tree's bark, as if it had been carved a long time ago and re-carved, time after time again.

AW + JC

Anne Weber, maybe? Perhaps JC was the hanged man. But how would I find out who this JC was? I took out my polaroid camera and snapped a picture of the carving. Then I decided to go back to the library and do some more digging through the old newspapers. Our town was small, and there were only three librarians, and it happened to be the same one as had been there the last time I was digging around for answers about the legend.

"What are you looking for today, Kathy?" she asked, noticing me poking around the old almanacs. I blushed. For some reason, I frequently felt secretive or insecure about whatever it was I was interested in.

"I'm looking for um, some more stuff on Anne Weber." I said, glancing off to the side sheepishly.

"Are you still looking into the hanging tree?"

I nodded.

"It's just a story, and Anne Weber is a coincidence. I don't think you'll find anything. At least, I can't think of anything else to give you."

"I understand, but look, I found this." I unzipped the small front pocket on my polaroid case and pulled out a small stack of photos. Right on the top was the picture I had taken of the initials. I handed it to the librarian, who at first looked a little confused.

"AW+JC. You think that the AW stands for Anne Weber?"

I nodded.

"Yeah, I think it really could be. Look at how deep the carving is. It's like somebody carved it a long time ago, and kept re-doing it as the years passed. It's too big a coincidence to just ignore. Anne Weber died there, and there are her initials on the tree, really deep."

The librarian handed me back the photo.

"Well, I can see how you would maybe make the connection. But something to understand, Kathy, is that the most mundane explanation is usually the true one. People like to make up scary stories, and sometimes there's a little shred of a true story buried inside. Most of the time though, that shred of the truth is it. It's just that a man being hung there is more dramatic than somebody drowning by accident."

"Yeah…" I said, unsatisfied. There had to be more to it than that. Of course, what the librarian said is very true, and as I've grown up, I've realized that more and more. But it wasn't like I was just married to the idea of finding the identity of this mystery hanging man, rather, my attention had shifted to the identity of the unknown person named "JC". Whether or not he was the hanging man, I wanted to know more about him.

Was he the one who carved the initials, or was Anne? Did he miss her terribly? Did he ever move on? The thought entered my head that he might even still be alive, albeit very old. I remember that I combed through the phone book, several times over, and looked for anyone with the initials JC.

I also rode my bike to the cemetery, on the advice of the librarian. She'd told me that if I wanted to know any more, I should look at Anne Weber's grave in the old part of the cemetery.

I'm not saying that you should put your nose in anybody's business, but to be honest I like the enthusiasm. Just be careful not to tread on anybody's private business.

I walked my bike down the footpath between aisles, looking for where the old graves were. I had been there before a few times, once I tried to find a ghost on Halloween night, but of course, there had been nothing. Nowadays, I'm thinking that my mistake was hanging around in the section with the most recent graves.

The plot with the old graves was a little overgrown, and many of the graves were covered in moss, or were so weather beaten that the names were worn and hard to read.

There were so many, and I started to wonder if it was worth looking for the proverbial needle in a haystack. When I was about to give up and turn back though, I spotted a grave that looked a little different from the others.

This grave didn't have as much moss as the others, and the grass around it was shorter in comparison. Somebody had also left flowers recently. As I approached, I was able to make out the lettering, which was much sharper than the lettering on the surrounding graves.

Anne Lucille Weber
September 8th, 1880- March 8th, 1904
John 3:16

For a moment, I couldn't believe that I had found her. I knelt down next to the grave and traced the letters with my finger. Somebody had been taking good, if infrequent, care of this grave. I looked around, as if there would be somebody around, flowers in hand and a dark umbrella over their head. Of course, there wasn't anyone but me out there.

All the classic books I'd ever read had taught me that somewhere in the graveyard, there must be a gravedigger with keys to the gate, a shovel on his shoulder, and a dark, mysterious past. One that connected to what I was looking for, of course.

After snapping a few pictures on my Polaroid, I went to the front gate and looked around for the toolshed, assuming that's where the gravedigger would be. I didn't find anyone around.

Promising myself that I'd come back, I rode my bike back home, stopping at the store for peanut butter like I'd promised my mom I would.

I was waiting in line with the peanut butter, and chocolate for me and me alone, when I got an idea.

There was a woman in line in front of me who was asking if they could restock an item that she always bought, some kind of soap.

"Well, we don't carry that kind anymore. It was expensive, and the owner didn't think enough people were buying it."

"Oh, I see. Well, that's the only dish soap that doesn't irritate my hands, and I don't want to drive all the way to Los Pajaros for it. Can the owner just order a little bit for me, and I'll pay extra?"

"I don't know, do you want me to ask when the owner gets back? I can leave a note on his desk so we don't forget."

That seemed to satisfy the woman, who left without making a fuss, thankfully.

After paying, I didn't go home. I put the jar in my backpack and ate my chocolate with one hand as I rode back up to the cemetery.

I found Anne Weber's grave again without any trouble and took out my composition book. I flipped to a blank page and wrote a note in my best, cleanest handwriting.

Hello whoever is cleaning this grave and leaving flowers. My name is Kathy Harbison and I'm 14 years old. I'm trying to solve a mystery about Anne Weber and JC. Please ask for me at the Plumdale Public Library. They'll know who I am and if it's okay with you I want to ask some questions.

To protect the note from March rain, I put it inside of my empty sandwich bag, and then put that under a rock to keep it from blowing away.

As I left, I kept looking behind me to make sure it was still there.

I didn't hear anything about the note for the rest of the week. I didn't dare ask the librarians if anyone had asked for me, but I suspect I might've if things had kept going the way they were.

However, my routine changed when I broke my arm.

My little sister loved birds, so my dad made her a wooden feeder. It was hung rather low, and my sister noticed that she couldn't watch them without scaring them away, so I offered to hang it up higher so they wouldn't be scared off when she wanted to watch them from the ground.

Like Icarus, I flew too close to the sun. If I'd stayed down by a few branches, I would've been fine, but I tried to get it higher, and the rather thin branch snapped.

Needless to say, I was a little distracted. When Barbara visited, she said I was lucky that I hadn't smashed my skull on the brick border of my mom's vegetable garden.

I had to take a few days off school, and didn't think much about my "project" until I decided to clean my backpack the afternoon before I went back.

My composition book was full of notes about the mystery, and I was looking them over- pretending I was a TV detective- when my dad knocked on my bedroom door.

"Kathy, were you expecting a call from the library? They called you to say that somebody inquired about your note?" he said, a note of confusion in his voice. It wasn't like I was hiding my investigation from my family, but I also didn't publicly advertise what I was doing.

"Is she still on the phone?" I asked, without directly addressing what my dad was silently asking.

"No, she had to go, but she said that you could come over when you want, and that somebody inquired about your note. Did you leave a note in a book, Kathy?"

I nodded.

"Yeah. It's just a thing. I wanted to see who the next person checking it out was. Just for fun." I said. That did seem like something I would do, and I wondered to myself why I hadn't done that before.

"Ah, okay." he started to close the door, but stuck his head back in to let me know that the librarian had said "get well soon".

I looked at the clock, saw that it was about an hour before the library closed, and climbed out of bed, slipping my shoes on. I didn't care that I was still in pajamas, and walked downstairs, my balance still adjusting to having one arm in a heavy cast.

"Are you going to the library?" my mom asked from the kitchen, leaning around to see me heading for the front door.

"Yeah, somebody found my book note." I said, hoping she wouldn't put a pin in my plans.

"Not today, honey. You can go after school tomorrow. If you're bored, then you can help your sister with her book report, she's been hitting her head against it all day."

"I won't be gone long, though." I said.

"Just humor me, okay? I don't want you falling off your bike and getting hurt worse."

I wondered what difference me going to school tomorrow would make in easing my mom's worries about me riding my bike, but I nodded and went upstairs to help Christy with her book report.

At school the next day, I was more popular than I had ever been before. Even people I barely knew were coming up and offering to sign my cast, and by the end of the day my arm was covered in different colored signatures and get well messages.

I wasted no time; as soon as the bell rang, I got on my bike and rode- wobbly at first- to the library.

"Hey," I said, walking up to the front desk. "You said that somebody asked about the note? The note in the-" I whispered the next part, "-*graveyard?*"

She nodded, and reached under the desk and handed me a small, folded piece of paper.

"Yes, she came in yesterday afternoon and said she was the sister of the person buried there."

My heart quickened.

"Really? The sister? Was she-" I stopped myself, but the librarian picked up on what I was about to say.

"She was pretty old, yeah. Gave her name as Mrs. Emily Dawson, her address is here. She asked me to give it to you so you two can talk."

I took the paper and unfolded it. She lived here in town, I could probably bike there. The street name was familiar.

"Thanks!" I said, and went over to this one wall near the entrance that had a map of the town framed on it. I glanced down at the note, and tried to find *497 Wisteria Way*. It was on the outskirts, near the forest that the river ran through. Not too far from the hanging man tree.

I put my backpack on a table nearby, and grabbed my notebook and a pencil. It was hard to keep the book from slipping as I wrote with just one arm free, but I was able to copy down the directions to Ms. Dawson's house.

"Thanks!" I called again to the librarian as I left. I couldn't hold the directions with one hand, so I had to stop every so often and take my notebook out again so I could be sure I was going the right way.

Twenty minutes after leaving the library, I stopped in front of a fancy and vintage looking two story house. It was one of the older houses in town, though it was kept in much better condition than a lot of the other ones. Looking at it, I actually kind of felt like I had gone back in time, and despite being on the edge of discovery, I stayed on the sidewalk for a few moments just looking at it. I had rode my bike past a lot of old houses in this part of town, houses that had "FOR SALE" signs on their overgrown lawns. They were so decrepit and run down though, that people barely bought them. I actually hadn't ever seen one renovated.

I liked to sneak into those old houses and explore them, even though there were warning signs on the doors saying that it wasn't safe to go in. As I walked up the little path through the well-tended lawn of this particular house, I wondered if it would have a similar layout to the ones I had snuck into before. I wondered if it would be familiar, in a weird way.

I hopped up the wooden steps to the shady porch, and looked around. Sometimes you can guess what sort of person someone is based on what their porch looks like. Even if I didn't already know that an old lady lived here, I would've guessed it was an old lady. There were little statues of white, fluffy cats standing on either side of the door, and the welcome mat had paws on it. There was a wreath of artificial flowers on the door surrounding the peephole, as well as a wooden sign that said *Jesus Lives Here.*
As the windchimes hanging over her potted plants sang, I finally knocked. I looked at the peephole, waiting to hear footsteps or something. I heard a muffled voice come from the inside, an old lady.

"Coming! Be right there."

I'm sure that it was less than a minute, but it took a little while before I heard slow, heavy footsteps approaching the door.

"Just a minute." I heard the voice say, as the footsteps got closer.

"No- no problem." I said, trying to sound friendly, but not in a door-to-door solicitor sort of way.

I heard a few locks being undone, and the door opened.

"Hello, are you Mrs. Dawson?" I asked, regarding the rather short old woman standing in the doorway with a cane. She had glasses with thick, plastic green rims, and long almost white hair that was tied up in a neat bun. She didn't seem surprised to see me.

"Why, yes. Do you happen to be Kathy Harbison?"

I nodded.

"Mmm hmm. That's me. I heard from the library that you asked about my note. The one on the grave."

"Come in." She gestured and let me into the house. When she closed the door it took my eyes a while to adjust to the dimmer lighting. I could see that the layout *was* similar to the houses I'd explored before, beginning with a hallway, the kitchen and dining room on one side and the living room on the other. I saw some pictures hanging on the wall. I saw a really old wedding photo, and I wondered if it was Mrs. Dawson getting married.

"Can I get you anything to drink?" she asked, walking slowly down the hallway. I had to purposefully slow down my pace.

"Um, maybe just some water."

We turned into the kitchen- the updated appliances, including a very modern fridge and oven, clashed a little bit with the old vintage table set and wallpaper.

"Thanks so much for having me." I said, watching her pour the water out of a pitcher that had been sitting on the counter.

"I was surprised to see a note there, but it's lovely to meet you." she said.

Ice cubes clanked against the sides of the glass as she handed it to me. Without saying much beyond random pleasantries about the weather, or my trip over was, we went to the living room. The furniture looked like something out of an antique shop, and I was a little nervous sitting down on an embroidered back chair, unable to shake the feeling that it would just collapse as soon as I sat down. Maybe she noticed how stiff I was sitting, because Mrs. Dawson spoke first.

"Now dear, you said that you were trying to solve a mystery. Something about Anne Weber?"

"Yeah. The librarian said that she was your sister." I hadn't been sure how I was going to approach the subject, Anne had died after all, and while I wanted to know the story, I also was afraid of seeming insensitive.

Mrs. Dawson picked up a mug that was on the coffee table and held it in both hands.

"Yes, Anne was my older sister. I also had two other older sisters, Carrie and Eliza, but Anne was the oldest. She always was looking out for us, though she was quite the romantic. Always daydreaming, always falling behind on things. Sometimes we had to give her a little prod." Mrs. Dawson said fondly. I smiled too.

"Either me or my grandson go to the grave every so often to leave flowers or clean it, that's how I found your note. Why are you interested in my sister?" she asked. She didn't sound annoyed or suspicious, just curious. I jumped at the opportunity to explain myself.

"Well, my friends and I tell a lot of stories at sleepovers, or when we're just eating lunch. They tell stories about this hanging man. An urban legend, you know? Like the hook-hand man, or bigfoot. Sometimes they say uh, that he was rejected by the woman he loved, sometimes they tell it like he was um…" I didn't want to say *possessed by Satan* in front of an old lady. "A very bad man who killed someone and hung himself because he felt guilty. There's so many variations on the story that it made me want to see if there was anything real about it. I did some research and digging around, and found out about your sister. I thought maybe there was a connection between her and the- the guy."

Mrs. Dawson's face betrayed nothing. She just nodded, as if to say *ah, I see.*

"In your note, you mentioned the initials JC. That would be Jeremy Coleman."

Jeremy Coleman, I thought. Finally, a name to go with the initials. The foggy mental image I had was slowly coming into focus.

Mrs. Dawson continued,

"Jeremy Coleman came to our town to work in his uncle's sawmill, and had taken up residence in my father's hotel. It doesn't exist anymore, the building it was in was used for apartments, but then it was knocked down. I believe there's a pizza parlor there now."

"Is it *Papa Giuseppe's*?" I'd been there many times with mom, dad, and Christy.

"That's the place." Mrs. Dawson said. "My sister Anne did a lot of cleaning. My family was rich, but at the time we had lost a lot of money, and so oftentimes me and my sisters had to work just as hard as our father did. I don't remember Anne ever complaining though, I think she thought it was romantic, like Cinderella or something."

"Is that how she met him?"

"Not exactly. Anne loved to draw, and sketching flowers was her favorite. The sawmill was near the woods where she would go off to draw sometimes, and one day he went out on his break to take a walk."

"That's a really cute way to meet." I said.

"I remember thinking that too. Anne and Jeremy hit it off right away, and she was so happy whenever she bumped into him in the hotel hallways. I saw them having coffee or tea in the dining room, always talking, always smiling and laughing about something. Of course, eventually our father caught on, and figured if Anne was enamored with this Jeremy boy, he might as well meet him formally. He invited him to dinner at our house, in the dining room over there." she pointed over at the hall, and even though I couldn't see the dining room from my seat, I turned my head to look anyway.

"Did it go well?" I asked. I knew that things couldn't end well, I already sort of knew how the story ended, but I still didn't have much background or context. Even if someone spoils the ending of a movie, it's still interesting to see how they get there, after all.

"It went reasonably well. Father asked him a lot of questions about his family, and Jeremy would either dodge the question, or answer it vaguely. His uncle owned the sawmill, his father was a lawyer, and he was from the city. Our father, he wasn't a terribly strict or stern man, but he wasn't sure about the match. So far as he could tell, Jeremy was a hard-worker, and a polite, responsible person. He liked that about him. He wanted to know more, though. Like you, our father was terrific at research and finding things out. I was twelve at the time so I can't be sure, but I'm fairly positive he had a detective look into him."

"That's pretty thorough." I remarked.

"Yeah. So, I noticed my sister and Jeremy getting closer. She didn't tell me and our other sisters everything, but I could just see from looking at them that they were completely wrapped up in each other. They went on walks, she always brought him food for his break at the sawmill, and he started joining our family at Sunday services. He would sit next to Anne, and sing the hymns so loudly. I thought he had an awful pretty voice. I think I might've had a crush on him, just a little bit, even though he and my sister were clearly in love."

"In love?" There is such a weight about that phrase.

"I believe it."

I folded my hands on my knees and frowned.

"So… what happened? It sounds like it was going so well."

"What happened is that Jeremy wanted to ask Anne to marry him, and he asked my father's permission. Now, please don't think that my father was an awful man, I know things are different nowadays. But he said no. He told Jeremy that he couldn't give him his blessing to propose to Anne."

"Why? He wasn't rich enough?"

Mrs. Dawson shook her head.

"No, I don't think it was that. See, I was sitting on the stairs, listening to them. They were talking in this room, and me and my sisters were supposed to be in bed. I heard their voices though, so I snuck down. So, our father wasn't angry with Jeremy, but he told him that he couldn't let him marry Anne. And Jeremy- I couldn't see his face, of course- but he seemed calm. He just asked why. My father told him what he had found out about him. I didn't hear everything. Some of the conversation was too low to hear from the stairs in the hall. What I gather is that father found out that Jeremy spent time in an asylum, one for well, we would call them troubled children. Something dreadful had happened to Jeremy when he was young, and it seemed to have been bad enough to make it so he needed to be institutionalized."

"Weren't those places awful?" I asked quietly.

"I'm not sure what it was like for him. All I know is that he was able to leave when he was grown up. Maybe he seemed like he'd improved, I don't really know. But that was why father wouldn't let him marry Anne."

"What happened then?"

"Nothing. Jeremy left, and he just avoided Anne altogether. I don't think she knew why. All I remember is that she was so dreadfully upset and wondered what she did wrong. I don't think father told her about what he had found out, or that Jeremy had asked him for permission to marry her. Anyway, a few weeks, or maybe a few months passed. Then, I think Anne found a letter on the doorstep one morning. She read it and dashed off without a word. I heard her calling his name. I tried to follow her, but I couldn't catch up. I found the letter in the grass. When I couldn't find Anne, I went to the hotel to find father and told him what happened. I don't remember much else, it's all kind of a blur. That afternoon is when things started to piece together. They found Anne in the river, and signs that she had slipped in the mud and fallen. You already know what happened to Jeremy." she said, gazing out into space. There was an awkward silence.

"That's why he did it? That's really sad." I wasn't sure what to say, and that was the best I could come up with. "What- what did you guys do? If it's okay to ask, I don't- I don't want to be-"

"We buried Anne. You know where. It was a lovely day, lots of flowers in bloom, she would've loved it. Jeremy's family, I think that they took him out of town. That's what I heard whispered around the town. You know, suicide was very hush-hush. I don't know where he was buried. My sister Carrie tried to find out, but I don't think she found anything. There wasn't any real information for closure, so rumors sprang up to fill the gap, I suppose."

She took a sip from her mug and put it back down with a slight clatter on the coffee table.

"The real thing isn't quite what I would call a campfire story, huh." she said.

"Yeah."

"Not really a story to tell with a flashlight under your chin."

"Do you think it's bad? That everyone tells stories?"

Mrs. Dawson was deep in thought for a moment before answering.

"Well, I don't think it's so bad. Kids always tell stories. I suppose it's only bad because nobody remembers who Jeremy was. He was a nice young man, one who would never hurt a fly. I suppose I wouldn't mind the stories if they would at least keep that part. But then again," she stood up, and I did too. "That hanging man from the stories, that isn't really Jeremy Coleman. It's just the hanging man."

***

The next week was my fifteenth birthday. I had two close friends, and that night we put up a tent in my backyard and as usual, had snacks and flashlights ready for spooky stories.

I hadn't told Barbara and Jennifer about my findings. I liked to sit on stuff until I was completely done. Anytime I had a project. Whether it was a drawing, or a story I was writing- anything. I liked to keep it to myself until I had something real special to show them. My notebook was sitting under my sleeping bag, and I was about to reach for it when Barbara held the flashlight under her chin.

"My big brother snuck me into a rated X movie at the theater during his shift yesterday. I missed the title, but I think it was called *You're Dead Meat*, it was *nasty*. You've never seen so much corn syrup splattering across a screen in your life. Generally, I liked it! But I did find a few plot holes that could have easily been fixed. Ladies, allow me to share the new and improved version of *You're Dead Meat*."

Me and Jennifer listened attentively, snacking on grapes and crackers as Barbara recounted her revised version of the plot, along with her loving descriptions of all the gore. I suspect she might've embellished it a little. Sometimes with gore, less is more, and the more juicy it gets, the less scary it gets, but I gave her points for effort.

"I can't believe you two are eating." she said when she was finished, twenty minutes later. She put the flashlight down on the pillow in the center of our little circle, and laid down on her side, propping her head on one arm. "Neither of you can top that, I bet."

"Well," said Jennifer. "I've got a story to share. My mom's reading this vampire novel, and I picked it up and read a little bit. I read the beginning, then skipped to the end. I didn't really like how it ended, I'd actually change a lot. Plus I'd change some of the vampire rules. You guys want to hear how *I* would end it?"

"Go for it!" I said.

I'd never read the book that Jennifer was retelling, but I have a feeling that her version deviated quite a bit. She packed quite a few plot twists into her fifteen minute story, and it ended in a double vampire wedding. I have to say, I think she might've been onto something there.

"That wasn't even scary. You *do* know that vampires are cannibals, right? You could've at least had Paul eat someone at his wedding." said Barbara.

"Well, I wasn't trying to be more gruesome than you, I was going more for something with heart. Y'know?"

"Eh, sure. How about you, Kathy?" Barbara asked.

"Yeah, you said you were working on something!"

I pulled my notebook out from under my sleeping bag. I remembered what Mrs. Dawson had told me before I left. The hanging man from the stories was his own character, and he'd had his fun. I wanted to tell the story of a random man from years ago, one who lay, turning to dust, in a plain grave that everyone forgot. Yeah, he's just one guy and Anne is just one girl, in a world of bigger and higher-stakes stories. But then again, our own stories are high stakes to us, aren't they? Even if our own problems and dramas don't amount to anything that changes the world.

"I've got one. It's not necessarily a flashlight story, but I did a lot of work to find it."

About the author

A native of California, Monica Mendoza is an author and flautist currently in the midst of graduate studies for a Master of Music degree. She loves literature, performing music, and playing video games.

Monica is also a nature enthusiast and plans on someday climbing Half Dome in Yosemite National Park.

www.ingramcontent.com/pod-product-compliance
Lightning Source LLC
Chambersburg PA
CBHW051316130726
47987CB00004B/1826